'Let's get one t
heard Eliot say.

'Your mother asked me if I would like a part..........
ship in the Village Surgery. She came to me, in
London. Believe it or not, that's the truth. I didn't
foist myself on her after you—'

'After you ditched me.' The words were ugly, but
they were oh, so true.

'Lauren, you have no idea what you're saying.'

'Of course I know what I'm saying. The next thing
is, you'll be telling me you did it for my own
good.'

'As a matter of fact, that's exactly what happened,
though I don't expect you to believe me!'

Carol Wood writes her Medical Romances based on personal experience of veterinary life, backed by her work in medical general practice and her ties with people in the animal world. Married to a water-colour artist and with three of her children now living on the south coast, she enjoys conservation of wildlife, reading and curio shops.

PERFECT PARTNERS

BY

CAROL WOOD

MILLS & BOON

*First published in Great Britain 1997
Harlequin Mills & Boon Limited,
Eton House, 18-24 Paradise Road, Richmond, Surrey TW9 1SR*

© Carol Wood 1997

ISBN 0 263 80003 2

*Set in Times 10 on 11 pt. by
Rowland Phototypesetting Limited
Bury St Edmunds, Suffolk*

03-9701-49450-D

*Printed and bound in Great Britain
by Mackays of Chatham PLC, Chatham*

CHAPTER ONE

THE water hit the windscreen with a sickening thwack.

Lauren groped frantically to adjust the wipers which seemed to be submerged in water and leaves and ground across the glass like sandpaper. Then everything cut out. Engine, lights, heater, the lot.

'Please start. . .please!' She twisted the ignition key back and forward until the chug-chug of the waterlogged engine faded beneath her fingers and nothing but the torrential rain broke the eerie silence around her.

'Mobile!' Lauren reached out to the empty passenger seat and even in the split second of hope knew it was hopeless. She was no longer in her dusty, bone-juddering Jeep but driving a sophisticated, Western-made saloon car, hired at Heathrow not more than two hours ago. So much for calling assistance in England! At least in Africa she'd had all the support services of the medical team if she broke down.

'Think!' She gritted her teeth, trying to focus on the present. 'I must be. . .where?' She wound down the window a fraction and felt a blast of icy October rain on her face. 'Somewhere near Smithey's Ford, I think.'

Just then the car seemed to move. The brake was on, wasn't it? Her fingers went frantically to check it. Still the car seemed to slide. Within seconds icy water gurgled around her ankles and up her jeans-clad legs and seeped through the material until it reached her knees. Then the slow, cold, all-embracing nightmare began as she realised she had driven into Smithey's Ford itself.

The car rocked precariously. Water poured in over the open window, funnelling its way into every crack

5

and corner. Desperately she tried to free herself from the safety belt but it was stuck. Her cry for help was lost in the splashing of water as it tumbled over her arms and curled around her body. The terrifying creak of the chassis sent her brain into numb panic. Fighting wildly for the last breath of air, she strained up her chin from the bubbling surface, but the whirlpool of water began to suck her down until her lungs seemed to burst as the nightmare went on and on.

Lauren tried to open her eyes.

Half of her expected to see white walls and white nets hanging around the bed, expected to hear the laughing, rolling African tongue of the ward auxiliaries. Then the other half remembered England and the water seeping up around her ankles and the dark, suffocating silence of the car going down.

If only she could sit up and stop this whirling sensation. . .

'Hey, take it easy!' A pair of hands restrained her.

She blinked hard, clearing her vision and, thankfully, part of her mind, remembering now the last few seconds before she had blacked out.

'Don't try to move; just take your time.'

Her eyes flicked up and into yet another bad dream. She was lying in her bed in her old room at Gorsehall Cottage and the man sitting beside her was Dr Eliot Powers, a man she despised with all her heart. Four years hadn't changed him at all, except to make him look more devastating than ever. His broad, muscular shoulders were clad in a thick grey fisherman's sweater and the brooding, beautiful sea-blue eyes, which shone like two brilliant beams, were still as piercing as ever under the head of thick, glossy black hair.

He swept a curious gaze over her. 'What happened? I found you in the middle of Smithey's Ford. Luckily the car you were in got stuck on a ledge—otherwise you might not have been so lucky.'

Lauren fought to remember, her head aching as she concentrated. 'I. . .I lost my way somehow. . .then suddenly water came pouring in the car. My belt wouldn't unlock—after that, I don't remember any more.'

'You little fool,' he growled at her. 'Why not tell me you were coming home? I would have come to meet you.'

Exactly what she had wanted to avoid! The less she had to do with Dr Eliot Powers the better, and she jerked her head away sharply from his gaze. 'You brought me here?'

'Where else would I take you?' His voice was low and gruff. 'You were out cold when I pulled you from the car. I got you home as quickly as I could before you froze to death.'

Lauren involuntarily put her hand to her mouth. She felt her pulse quicken as she touched her lips. 'I r-remember something. . .someone leaning over me?'

He nodded. 'I gave you mouth-to-mouth and you brought up half of Smithey's Ford.'

She groaned, the memory fuzzy. His lips covering hers, his hands on her body. . .

She blinked, swallowing, staring down at the unfamiliar black towelling robe pulled around her. 'Where are my clothes?'

'Drying.' He calmly returned her horrified glare. 'You were underwater. Come on, Lauren, don't look so shocked. I'm a doctor, remember?'

Contempt filled her green eyes. 'How could I ever forget?'

He rose to his feet, letting his breath out in a long sigh. 'In your present mood—and condition—I suggest we save a debacle until you're feeling fitter. Suffice it to say you'd better get some rest. I'm downstairs if you

want me. I'm on call. . .so I might have to leave at any
point. If you need anything—'

'I shan't,' she muttered, pulling the bedcovers
around her.

'Very well.' He hesitated briefly, then pulled open
the door. 'We'll talk in the morning.'

Lauren felt the blood drain from her face as he left.
The damp fronds of her dark hair curled down onto the
thick towelling robe, reminding her that he must have
stripped her, dried her and redressed her. This was his
robe, she supposed, fingering it with a shudder, a quiver
of sensation running through her as she sniffed the
musky aftershave on its black fibres.

Exhausted, she felt herself sinking into the pillows.
Thoughts crowded her mind as she closed her eyes.
Thoughts that she had successfully managed to erase for
the last four years came tumbling back, one after another,
as though the floodgates of her mind were suddenly
opened: the busy London hospital where she had trained,
her high hopes of becoming a surgeon and that last year
when she had met Eliot Powers and fallen so deeply in
love—the year when her life had seemed so full and
promising at one moment and then so bitterly dis-
appointing the next.

Finally she fell into a fitful sleep, only to be woken
by her own voice crying out, her body bathed in sweat.
Her hair fell limply over her face and was as wet as her
soaked forehead beneath.

Light suddenly bathed the room and arms threaded
themselves around her, holding her still as her body
convulsed. 'It's all right. . .it was just a dream,' Eliot's
voice soothed.

Her eyes met his face and then over his shoulder she
saw with relief the familiar shelves of books and the
lattice window under the eaves. He folded her trembling

body into his arms and held her to him, pressing her head against his chest.

'F-for a minute I thought it was Mother,' she found herself stammering weakly.

He moved her hair from her wet eyes with large hands and held her as she collected her thoughts and knew this was the reason she was home—that her mother was dead.

All those weeks of lying in the Tropical Disease Centre knowing she was too ill to fly home and attend the funeral, too ill even to write or let anyone know. . . all those long days and nights. . .

'That's it. . .sleep, now.' His voice seemed a long way off, but she felt his fingers kneading into the tight muscles of her shoulders and with a sigh she relaxed as his hands came up to stroke her hair on the pillow, and finally she gave way to the waves of warmth that slowly engulfed her.

She felt something brush her cheek as she lapsed into the last shadow of consciousness, then she fell heavily asleep, unaware of the careful hands moving over her utterly fatigued body to remove the soaked sheet and replace it with a fresh, crisp, clean one.

Sunday morning dawned. The storm was over.

A tall, willowy girl, Lauren possessed nothing much to speak of in curves. Now she stretched her slender body and felt its achingly lean joints, sensitive to the English winter and the freezing water which had enveloped her yesterday. It all seemed like a ghastly nightmare. Already she was missing the intensive vaccination programme and the sun-filled warmth of the continent she had left behind.

She was grateful to Africa. It had successfully swallowed up the last two years of her life and obliterated the unhappy memories of her love affair with Eliot

Powers—but now she was home and she must start to rebuild her life and the practice that she had inherited from her mother.

It seemed that Eliot Powers, however, remained a continuing problem—but not for long, she decided resolutely, making one more effort to sit up.

She tried to push up her slender frame in the tousled bed and sighed defeatedly; the heat and the malaria she had contracted had honed down her figure to sylph-like proportions and she realised that unless she got some carbohydrate inside herself she was likely to pass out again.

'Feet first,' she sighed, and slipped them down to the floor. A wave of dizziness rushed over her—a legacy from the malaria, she wondered briefly, or perhaps Smithey's Ford?

Breathing in deeply, she made her way to the *en suite* shower and propped herself under the warm water. Taking her time, she dried her hair, fluffing it out to its former silkiness, and slipped on navy jogging pants and sweater from her wardrobe. Then she took the familiar old stairs one by one, bending her head carefully under the oak beams of the house.

When she walked into the drawing room Eliot was making a fire, bending down to set the logs alight. He stood up when he saw her and smiled. 'Good morning. How do you feel?'

She sat down by the open hearth, grateful for the warmth that suddenly sprang into life amidst the logs. 'Better, thanks.'

'You need some breakfast inside you.'

'Yes, perhaps. . .' Her voice trailed off as she saw that he had already prepared a tray of eggs, toast, juice and a pot of coffee.

'Eat up.' He slid it on to the coffee-table beside her.

She looked up at him, her green eyes wary. 'We have to talk.'

'Indeed we must. But finish that first.'

She did as she was told and found the eggs perfectly cooked. The soft centres slid down easily, washed down by the juice and freshly ground coffee. By the time she had finished, he had persuaded the fire into a full blaze. She took her tray out, feeling stronger, wandering into the kitchen to breathe in the aroma.

Her mother had loved this kitchen. They'd spent many hours in it together and she was pleased to have those memories. But she must also keep them in perspective, for it was the future now that she had to concentrate on. She moved slowly through the other rooms, identifying familiar objects, pleased to feel the old house welcome her with its warmth and snugness.

When she returned to the drawing room Eliot's brooding figure lounged in one of the leather fireside chairs, dressed in a thick white Aran sweater, his long, cord-covered legs stretched out in front of him.

'I've asked Ken Howard, your family solicitor, to come over,' he told her as she took the chair opposite. 'He should arrive any minute.'

She nodded. 'I heard from him briefly in Mombasa. I understand he was appointed executor of Mother's will?'

He frowned, tilting his dark head. 'If you heard from him in Mombasa, why didn't you reply?'

Lauren stiffened, her green eyes cool. 'I'll discuss my reasons with Ken when I see him. As for the situation here, if you will let me know how soon you will be leaving, then I can make the necessary arrangements to advertise for a locum.'

'As for the situation here,' he mocked her, 'don't you think you owe Hugo and me some explanation as to why we haven't heard a word from you? Who do you think has kept things running smoothly in your absence. . .?

Heaven's above, Lauren, three months! Where the hell have you been?'

She stared defiantly at him, trading glare for glare. 'If it was so inconvenient for you to manage the practice until I returned home, why stay? I'm sure Hugo could have brought in a locum until I arrived.'

'That's hardly the point!' He stood, blue eyes blazing at her taunt. 'Hugo had his own problems to contend with. All you could think about was gadding around the universe, doing your good deeds for mankind. You couldn't have given a damn about what was going on here!'

'How dare you?' she gasped indignantly. 'If circumstances prevented me from coming home—'

'Circumstances?' he derided her angrily. 'You had a funeral to attend and a practice to run. Tell me, just how long does a flight from Africa take these days?'

She willed her voice to keep steady. 'I will not be interrogated like this!'

'I'm just asking for a little directness, that's all,' he responded bitterly, evidently as angry as she was. 'But directness was never your best point, was it, Lauren? You'd rush off somewhere and make yourself distinctly unavailable rather than confront a problem. My God, I would have thought you'd have grown up by now, that your missions of mercy would have taught you something about life you obviously haven't understood before.'

She stood up herself, her green eyes blazing. 'Grow up, you say? If I was so repulsively immature why the hell did you go to bed with me? Or did seducing me make just another conquered heart to add to your considerable list of drooling students?'

Immediately she had said it, she wanted to retract it. In saying those words she knew she had revealed that she still hurt, and the signs of heartache must still be etched somewhere on her face.

'So. . .that's what all this is really about,' he breathed, his voice husky with contempt. 'You're still holding a grudge. That's why you haven't been in touch, isn't it?'

Her fingers curled angrily into fists at her sides as her cheeks flushed. 'I refuse to discuss the past with you. It's over and done with. What I want to talk about is the future and my plans for the practice.'

'Your plans!' he exclaimed bitterly.

'I'm prepared to buy you out. I'm prepared to pay you whatever you want for your share. Just name your price.'

He stared at her in disbelief, his jaw working, the tiny muscles clenching as the full meaning of what she had said became clear. Lauren waited, her heart banging so painfully in her throat that she could barely swallow. She hadn't meant it to come out like this, but it was done now.

'You must be joking.' His tone was low and incredulous. 'Buy me out, you say? Why the hell would I want you to buy me out?'

'Because it's quite clear a partnership between us wouldn't work,' she responded instantly, unable to imagine that he, too, didn't want a dissolution of the partnership. All her instincts had told her that he would jump at the opportunity of such an offer.

But he shook his head slowly, saying each word with terrifying emphasis so that she could be in no doubt as to his meaning. 'Now you listen to me for once. Hugo, your mother and I were all equal partners. Equal. I've worked hard here to build the practice up and you'll discover the practice is as much mine as it is yours. I suggest you talk to Ken before you try throwing your weight—or your money around.'

She was so shocked that she could hardly speak. 'I. . .I

think you'd better go,' she choked out, straightening her spine.

He almost laughed at her, throwing back his head. 'Go where exactly?'

She tilted up her chin, defying him with her eyes. 'I want you to move your things out of this house today. My mother extended you her hospitality—which you abused by staying on here as her guest for far too long. Now I'll thank you to find accommodation elsewhere. I'm sure there will be plenty of comfortable alternatives in the village whilst you decide your future.'

Two black eyebrows quirked up mockingly at her. 'You've got a lot to learn, Lauren. I suggest you defer your attempted annihilation of my existence until your discussion with Ken is over.'

He shouldered past her and strode out of the room with a cutting indifference. The air left behind was thick with animosity and yet there was something else too, she realized, stunned at her physical response to his presence as he'd swept past her. There was still that snap of electricity which had crackled between them during the last year of her training and had brought them together in such a passionate affair at St Margaret's.

At this moment it was manifesting itself in pure aggression, but beneath the surface there was something else—something far more dangerous to her than the anger of their quarrelling.

Suddenly, it was as if it were yesterday and her thoughts flew back to St Margaret's and to the doctor who had been assigned the dubious privilege of demonstrating anatomy to students at the busy London hospital. She had been just one of a handful of impressionable young acolytes who'd worshipped his every move. He'd been the sexiest-looking man she had ever seen and he'd swept her off her feet the moment she'd gazed into those hypnotic blue eyes.

The fact that neither of them had been able to ignore the growing attraction between them had resulted in a crazy, smouldering affair and she had fallen head over heels in love with the man who'd filled her thoughts both day and night and who she had imagined loved her. She had even brought him home to meet Mother!

From everyone else, they'd tried to keep the affair quiet. Student-doctor romances were strictly taboo. But falling in love had seemed so perfectly natural, until that terrible day at the end of the year when her world had collapsed. Not only had he quite ruthlessly told her he did not consider her surgeon material, but two weeks later he had dumped her like yesterday's old newspapers.

Mind-blown, she had continued in medicine only because she had had no alternative. She had lived like an automaton—eaten, drunk, breathed because she had to. And she'd qualified—just. Then the dean of the training school had found her a pre-registration post as a house physician in another hospital and the move had given her a precious breathing-space to lick her wounds.

When she had bumped into Eliot again at hospital functions she'd forced herself to pretend she was as careless of him as he had been of her. Even to her mother she had passed the affair off casually. But the strain had become too much. In the end, she'd jumped at the offer of work abroad with the World Health Organisation and within a few months she had found herself in Mombasa.

And that was when the worst thing had happened.

In her absence, Eliot Powers, trading on their friendship, had somehow persuaded her mother to take him on as a third partner in the practice. The news had reached her one day in a brief letter, long after it had been written, the letter having been diverted from a dozen different addresses within the vaccination programme.

She had been totally devastated. As it had been too late for her to write back and warn her mother of the kind of person he really was, she had been forced to accept the situation. Just thinking of Eliot Powers under her mother's professional roof had been bad enough— but to hear he was also living at the cottage as her mother's guest. . .!

She blinked hard, coming back to the present, more aware than ever that she had allowed herself to be taken in once before. She would never allow it again.

Just then a Mercedes pulled into the drive and she glimpsed Ken Howard alighting, acknowledging Eliot who appeared to be leaving. She felt a brief moment of triumph. At least he would be out of the house whilst she talked to Ken.

She sank back, feeling suddenly exhausted. This fight would cost her every ounce of strength, but she was determined. She hated to think of him under Gorsehall's roof, let alone the surgery's. Surely there would be some legal manoeuvre she could employ to force him into relinquishing his share?

Ken Howard walked in and held out a firm hand and her spirits rose. If anyone could provide a solution, Ken would. A tall man in his late fifties with slightly receding hair, he had known her since she'd been a child.

He kissed her cheek. 'Good to see you after so long, my dear.'

'You too, Ken. Thank you for coming out on a Sunday.'

He smiled. 'Not at all.' They sat and he said gently, 'My condolences, Lauren. A heart attack was the last thing we expected.'

Lauren swallowed and nodded. 'Thanks, Ken.'

As if reading her thoughts the solicitor said kindly, 'Don't feel badly that you were away when it happened. Susan was happy for you to have the valuable experience abroad. . .although she always hoped one day you'd follow her into general practice.'

Lauren sighed. 'Yes, she did, didn't she? But I need to take stock of things, Ken,' she added softly. 'General practice would have seemed like a strait-jacket to me once, but not now. Things have changed.'

He nodded slowly, looking at her thoughtfully. 'Did you receive her last letter, by any chance?' he asked as he removed a sheaf of documents from his briefcase and spread them on the table.

'Letter? No.'

'Oh, dear. Eliot found it after she'd died. He was in two minds whether to hang onto it, but decided to send it on to you.'

Lauren sighed again. 'All right, I'll make some enquiries. The post was non-existent sometimes. When it did reach us it was always weeks or months late. I only received the Mombasa letter because I was in Mombasa at the time of delivery.'

He nodded and began to lift the paper to read. 'Well, down to business, my dear. It is quite short business, I have to say. Short and to the point. As her only child— indeed, as the only surviving relative—you are the beneficiary of your mother's estate. I'm sure you're aware of that.'

Lauren listened with a heavy heart. And what she heard didn't surprise her. A few personal bequests to friends and neighbours, a donation made to a local hospital, but she, Lauren, to inherit the remainder of the estate and her mother's interests and partnership in the Village Surgery, as it was known. Ken Howard read over the legal terms, and then landed his bombshell.

'Lauren, your mother invested the proceeds from the sale of Gorsehall Cottage in the refurbishment of the surgery.' Ken Howard frowned, staring in concern at Lauren's white face. 'You are aware, I suppose, she sold this house?'

All Lauren could do was shake her head, her mind a

total blank. 'I. . .I don't believe it. There must be some mistake, Ken.'

He shook his head. 'It happened a year ago. I would have thought Susan would have written to you.'

Lauren rose sharply to her feet. 'But nothing would have made her sell Gorsehall!'

The solicitor picked up the documents he had taken from his briefcase, sighing deeply. 'I think you had better study these, Lauren. They are from the sale of the house.'

She just couldn't believe it. She took the papers and stared blindly at them. A single signature stood out, one which was engraved on her heart.

'Eliot Powers?' she breathed, staring at the long, sprawling signature, blinking her eyes as if that would erase the sight of it. 'But it can't be.'

The solicitor looked at her with sympathy. 'Lauren, your mother refused to discuss the sale of Gorsehall with me. I'm afraid there's nothing I can tell you other than what you see before your eyes.'

'But why, Ken? Why?' she persisted incredulously, shaking her head.

'I honestly don't know, my dear. Perhaps you had better ask the only man who can enlighten you. Eliot himself.'

Lauren looked up, numbly taking in the room around her with its comfortable solidity, the room she loved best of all in the house, where she could remember having sat in front of the open fire with her father when she was very small, before he'd died.

Eliot Powers! That man had so much to answer for. She could barely contain herself until she saw him again.

CHAPTER TWO

THE opportunity came sooner than she expected.

Almost immediately Ken had left, Eliot rang.

'Lauren—'

She cut him short, abandoning the resolution to keep her temper the moment she heard his voice. 'Why didn't you tell me?' she demanded, still trembling.

He was silent for a moment. Then she heard him say evenly, 'If you'd given me a chance to explain—'

'What is there to explain?' she interrupted angrily. 'Nothing is going to change the fact that somehow you tricked my mother into selling you this house.'

'Tricked?' he barked back. 'What are you talking about?'

'You used our friendship to ingratiate yourself into the practice and then you decided it was not enough. She would never have parted with the cottage unless she was—'

'For God's sake, just shut up a moment!' The phone crackled under her ear. 'You'll have your chance to crucify me later. All I'm asking you to do now is come and help. It's Viner's Stables. Do you know it?'

She forced back her anger in a hard swallow, snapping her jaws so hard that she heard her teeth crunch. 'Of course I know it. I used to ride with the Drummonds when I was younger.'

'Well, a telegraph pole has come down and smashed the house up. People are hanging around here in shock and Hugo can't come because he's on call this weekend and out somewhere. There's a spare case on the refectory table and the keys to your mother's Saab are hanging in

19

the kitchen cupboard on the board. I expect to see you here in ten minutes at the most.'

The act of finding her way to the kitchen cupboard, selecting the keys which had Saab plainly written on the tag and collecting the spare case and then opening up the garage in the garden barely lessened the cocktail of emotions going on inside her. Fury towards him because of what Ken's visit had revealed compounded the anger at his demanding her presence in the way he had. But she had to put it all from her mind now. There were obviously people needing help badly and she must get there as swiftly as possible.

Only once before had she seen the Saab, her mother's new investment just over two years ago. Blessing the fact that it held no special memories for her, she unlocked it, jiggled her way through the gears and found neutral before switching on.

It burst into life first time. She drove through the familiar lanes of the New Forest leaving the village, clunking the gears until she was familiar with them. The stables were well-known for its lengthy hacks over the heathland where she had ridden as a child, although since then the Drummonds had retired and the relatively new owners were only vaguely familiar to her.

Lauren gasped when she saw the state of the place— trees down, huge, muddy lakes of water surrounding the empty stables and, worst of all, a telephone pylon shedding its tentacles across the roof of the main house.

As she pulled up, an ambulance crew were lifting in two people on stretchers. Firemen were trying to deal with the pylon and the police had cordoned off the house. She finally discovered Eliot bending over huddled figures sitting on bales of straw beside the main stables. 'What happened?' She pulled off her anorak and threw it across a fence and he looked up at her, his brow furrowed in concentration.

'God knows. The pylon came down and Viner's lad broke a leg, caught under falling masonry. They hauled him out and his sister too. She's OK, but she needs X-rays on her ankle. Mum's gone in the ambulance with them but there are two youngsters who came out for rides sitting in my car over there. Then there's George Viner. I don't know where the hell he's disappeared to.'

Lauren nodded, watching the way he gently bound the wrist of the young stable lad. Her heart suddenly drove against her ribs in a pang of remembrance as she saw the strong fingers binding the wound, the motion as familiar to her today as it had been four years ago, when they'd moved over her in much the same way, gentle and caressing, and it sent an unbidden surge of desire leaping under her skin, forcing her to take a sharp breath.

'Is the house off bounds?' she asked quickly.

He nodded. 'The pylon demolished part of the roof and severed some electricity cables—virtually electrified the house. What with the water all over the place from the storm it's like a time bomb in there.'

Lauren left him and pushed her way through the team of rescue workers. She made her way to the dark blue Rover that Eliot had indicated. In it sat two teenage girls, fairly shocked and suffering from minor cuts and abrasions. Satisfied they had no more than superficial wounds, Lauren tended to them, then turned her attention to the man sitting on an animal-food sack.

'Mr Viner? I'm Lauren Kent, Dr Susan Kent's daughter. I think we've met once or twice in the village, haven't we?'

He looked up at her with glazed eyes. 'I. . .I just don't know what happened,' he mumbled. 'It was all so quick. The pole came down and lit the house up like a firework.'

Lauren set down her case. 'Let's have a look at the damage, shall we?' She could see that his hands were

burnt and, helping him to remove his coat, she discovered extensive bruising and lacerations on his arms.

'How did you get these? From the pole?'

'I'm not sure,' he replied vaguely.

'Can you remember if you received a shock?' She
tried to clean the worst of the wounds, noting that at
least one of them needed stitching.

'Something knocked me down. It's all a bit hazy.'

Lauren examined his eyes, head and reflexes, then
noticed an abrasion to the left of his ear. 'I really think
it might be better if you went to hospital, Mr Viner.'

'No!' He shook his head firmly. 'I must stay here.
Got to get the horses back in the stables.'

'You won't be able to do that until the place is found
to be safe.'

'But the lads won't be able to keep them horses out
in the field for much longer. It's like a bog.'

Lauren was certain the whole place had turned into a
quagmire, but her patient wouldn't help himself or his
horses if he had suffered any internal damage. 'Mr Viner,
you may have concussion,' she tried again. 'And if
you've had a shock—an electric current entering your
body somehow—then we need to check you out. You
may, for example, have hit your head, because there's
a considerable lump behind your ear. Plus that arm needs
stitching—'

'I'm not going to hospital!' he refused stubbornly.

She realised she was getting nowhere. 'Look, we'll
compromise. 'I'll take you into surgery and clean you
up and stitch that wound. Then you can come back
and sort out your horses, by which time the emergency
services will have everything under control.'

George Viner tried to stand up, wobbled and slumped
back down on the food sack. Defeated at last, he gave
a sigh, reluctantly nodding.

Lauren swiftly packed her case and made her way

back to Eliot. 'I'm not happy about George Viner,' she explained hurriedly. 'He won't go in to hospital, but he will come to the surgery at a push.'

'Can you cope?'

She nodded. 'I need keys, of course.'

He paused, then dug into his pocket, frowning at her for a moment. 'Perhaps you should know before you. . .' He hesitated, obviously reluctant to let her go, then shrugged. 'Well, never mind; you'll find out soon enough anyway.' He finally dropped the keys into her hand. 'I'll hang on here and get across to you as soon as we know there are no more casualties.'

She wondered what other time bomb he had been going to detonate, but in the second she was about to pursue the point he walked away and was soon absorbed in conversation with a policeman. Deciding she had better get back to George Viner, she dropped the keys in her case, then she helped Mr Viner to the Saab and drove to the village, wondering what lay ahead.

It wasn't long before she found out.

Taking a sharp left at the crossroads, she caught her breath as she drew up at the Village Surgery. Had it not been for the red brick and solid oak door of the façade, she might well have driven past. An extension had been added and, though in keeping with the traditional lines of the old, half-timbered building, it had at least doubled the practice in size.

It was a moment or two before she opened her door and got out, letting her eyes absorb the changes. Once inside the building she was only marginally aware of George Viner following her and her eyes couldn't seem to take everything in at once. She hoped at least for the familiar smell of her youth, the mixture of disinfectant and wood polish which had always pervaded the air, but even the smells had changed. Now the place was refurbished with soft blue couches and the once smoky

grey walls were a pristine white against the revitalised
oak beams.

She took in her breath at the blemishless rooms that
led off right and left. As she pushed the door open to
the first her eyes fell in astonishment on the diagnostic
ultrasound equipment. The next rooms offered similar
surprises; cryosurgery probe, state-of-the-art lighting,
respiratory spirometers and nebulisers, even electronic
acupuncture!

'Ah. . .Doctor?'

Lauren spun around. 'Oh, Mr Viner, I'm sorry,' she
gasped, remembering he was there. 'Let's go find ourselves a consulting room.'

They wandered back into the hall and to a room
marked 'Small Ops Room'.

She led him to a consulting table and helped him
remove his clothes. Then she browsed around, found
everything she needed to hand and washed at the brand-
new sink. Donning surgical apron and gloves, she turned
back to George Viner and took a breath.

The deepest cut on the right arm needed to be stitched,
which proved no problem with the efficiently prepared
suture trolley. Injecting lignocaine, she waited for the
area to go numb, absorbing more of her surroundings as
she did so.

'Yell at me if you can feel anything,' she told him,
and made the first suture. Her patient lay quietly, not
seeming to register her movements as she tied each stitch
off neatly. 'In a week you can have them out,' she told
him, eliciting no more than a nod. 'This smaller wound
won't need stitching. I'll clean it for you and you must
keep it dirt free. You'll also need a booster tetanus if
you haven't had one in the last few years. You're a
patient here, I take it?'

He frowned. 'It must be a dozen years since I came
to the doctor. Don't have the time for being ill.'

'I'm glad to hear it.' she smiled. 'But wounds like this have to be treated properly. The bacteria can multiply rapidly in dead skin or muscle. Toxin produced by the bacteria could attack the spinal cord nerves and then. . .well, let's just say a simple tetanus shot can save so much trauma.' She would have liked to add that she had spent a year trying to convince dozens of African villagers of just that fact, but very often the sight of syringes had frightened the native population, who'd preferred remedies from the local shaman. However, George Viner looked the last person to be interested in her advice this morning.

Just then a movement came from outside and Eliot appeared at the door. 'I see you've found your way around.'

Lauren nodded. 'Mr Viner requires a tetanus—and I think you might want to talk to him about his injuries,' she responded stiffly.

Eliot came over and pulled up a chair. His voice was calm and deep and a tingle of *déjà vu* travelled down her spine, making her hesitate for a second to listen. Then, realising she was gaping stupidly at his broad back, she relegated the debris to the bin, washed her hands and went off to continue her journey through the rest of the practice.

Having seen enough to identify Eliot's handiwork, she finally found her way to her mother's old room. This, too, had changed. New desk, comfortable padded patient chairs, a computer and glossy white walls. Years ago, they had reflected an ancient primrose yellow, the chairs had been the plastic type with springy backs and there had been homely curtains and nets at the windows.

Repressing a sharp pang of nostalgia, Lauren closed the door behind her and walked back to Reception where she discovered Eliot waiting, hands in pockets, leaning against the desk. His black hair was ruffled, and his blue eyes narrowed as she approached him.

'Where's George?' she asked, looking around.

'In my car. He wants to get back to the stables to sort out his darned horses.'

Lauren pulled her anorak around her, shivering suddenly. 'Well, I suppose there's not a lot more we can do if he's determined.'

He lifted himself from the desk and had begun to walk to the door when he stopped abruptly and frowned at her. 'So, what's the verdict?'

Lauren stiffened her spine. 'On the surgery? I almost drove past it. I would have appreciated a word of warning.'

He seemed to hesitate, but then merely shrugged. 'I really didn't know how much you knew—and I didn't want another row at the Viners'. If you had let me know you were coming home—'

'What would you have done? Waved a magic wand and put the surgery back as it was?' She sighed deeply, staring at him, trying to read an answer in his eyes. 'What did you do to make her sell you the cottage, Eliot? Why couldn't you have stayed out of my life— and hers?'

A deep frown sprang across his forehead. 'Is that what you would have wanted?'

'What do you think?' she gasped in amazement. Did he really not know how much he had hurt her all those years ago?

'You were in Africa. As far as I understood it, there was never any likelihood that you wanted to go into general practice in Gorsehall.'

She tossed back her head with a snarl of disgust. 'How dare you assume to predict my future?'

'I wasn't thinking of your future. You seemed to have it all worked out pretty well for yourself. I was thinking more of your mother, who was struggling to keep afloat and needed help.'

'That's absurd. She had my help. If she had needed it she would have asked me.'

'But you weren't here, were you?' He stared at her and she took a gulp, as she knew only too well that she hadn't been around when her mother had probably needed her, though, as far as she knew, she had been in good health, and had shown no signs of illness the last time she had seen her.

The faint, curling whisper of sickness that had begun in the pit of her stomach now grew heavier and she recognised the aftermath of the malaria as it took the energy quite suddenly from her legs. For a moment she reached out, trying to save herself, and then she seemed to sink, just as she had in the water yesterday, into the cold, deep blackness.

'How do you feel?'

She blinked, groping to breathe air into her lungs. 'I. . .I'm all right.'

'Inhale slowly; that's it.'

She was lying on one of the new couches and Eliot had her head in the crook of his shoulder. He was stroking her hair, his fingers smoothly taking its thickness back from her face.

'After Smithey's Ford it's no wonder you fainted. I shouldn't have dragged you out today.'

'I. . .I just need some air, that's all,' she mumbled, struggling to sit up. 'I'll be fine. It was a bit stuffy in here.'

He helped her to stand and she found herself wanting to explain about the malaria, but it all seemed just too much at the moment, besides which, he would probably think it was an excuse she was manufacturing for not having got home in time for the funeral.

'Look, come in my car and we'll drop off George, by which time you should be feeling better, and then I'll drive back here and you can pick up the Saab.'

She nodded, feeling too wobbly to protest, and eventually they got to the car, where she saw that George was looking as shattered as she felt. Eliot helped her into the back seat, returned to lock the surgery and then drove back out to the stables.

The pylon had been craned away from the roof at least. Eliot got out and chatted with the fire officers and policemen and, without bidding her goodbye, George Viner shambled out of the car, determined to get to his horses.

Eliot climbed back in. 'Do you think you're fit to drive home if I take you back to the Saab?'

'What home?' she muttered grimly as she met his gaze. 'According to Ken, I haven't got one. I'll pick up the Saab and collect my things from the cottage and find somewhere to stay in the village.'

'Don't be so bloody stupid!' This was the only remark he made as he turned to grind on the ignition. After that they travelled in silence and when they arrived at the surgery she got out of the Rover on unsteady but determined legs and made her way to the car. He followed her back to the cottage and every now and then she caught sight of him behind the wheel, driving the Rover in a steady course behind her.

It had grown chilly by the time they arrived at the cottage and Lauren felt shaky still as she got out of the car and looked up at the house. The eaves were full of leaves and the lattice windows glinted beneath them like little stars. She knew it all by heart, and wondered what it would feel like when she was forced to leave it for ever.

'I think we'd better talk,' Eliot said as he came to stand beside her.

'About what? I think it's all been said, hasn't it?' She

went to step forward and almost fell and he caught her, his strong arm slipping around her small waist.

'You're going to listen to some sense,' he muttered, and she was startlingly aware of the hard body on which she was relying for support as he drew her into the porch and jammed his key in the lock. 'Whether you like it or not.'

And she had the nasty suspicion that she was going to listen, whatever protest she made, though whether it was what she wanted to hear she seriously doubted.

'Drink up.' Eliot pushed the balloon glass into her hand and tipped the brandy to her lips.

She sniffed it and wrinkled her nose. 'Smells dreadful.'

'Well, it might, but at this moment you need something to warm you up.'

She drank a little, clutched her throat and gasped. 'It tastes like firewater.'

'Poison, of course,' he muttered cryptically, and slumped down opposite her, giving her a long stare. 'If your opinion of me is as low as I think it is, then obviously I'd be trying to kill you off rather than return you to the land of the living with a shot of good old-fashioned brandy.'

She pursed her full mouth. 'That's not funny.'

'It wasn't meant to be.'

She reluctantly sipped, contained the fire in her throat with a shudder and lowered the glass to the coffee-table he had pushed beside her on the old leather settee. Over her legs lay a warm blanket which he'd wrapped under her ankles, the fire was blazing and she felt her nose was lighting up like a beacon after the good weep she had had. A box of men's tissues lay on her lap and she took one and gave a blow.

'There will be things you need to ask me,' he said

suddenly, lifting a black brow. 'Where do you want me to start?'

'At the beginning would be a good idea,' she mumbled, blowing her nose again. 'Except that you can't change facts and the facts are that you now own Gorsehall and a third share in my practice.'

'*Your* practice?' he repeated cynically with an empty laugh, shifting his large body in the big fireside chair. Her eyes flicked over the supple leg, the long calf and foot she remembered so well. He was so complete. So confident and contained. Shoulders under the sweater filled the back of the chair and long arms lay casually, fingers drooping over the sides. Brown fingers. Artistic, skilled, experienced. Her mind whirled as memories tumbled through her mind of those caressing fingers smoothing her skin, drawing soft whorls of pleasure down her spine. . .

'Let's get one thing straight,' she heard him say, and she snapped back into the painful present. 'Your mother asked me if I would like a partnership in the Village Surgery. I didn't come here begging or pleading. She came to me, in London. Believe it or not, that's the truth. I didn't foist myself on her after you—'

'After you ditched me.' The words were ugly, but they were oh, so true.

'Lauren, you have no idea what you're saying.'

She was suddenly incensed. Did he take her for a fool? 'Of course I know what I'm saying. It's you who is trying to distort the truth. The next thing is, you'll be telling me you did it for my own good.'

'As a matter of fact, that's exactly what happened, though I don't expect you to believe me.'

'You're right, I don't,' she muttered, aware that he was staring at her with an expression that did the most incredible things to her system even though she was trying hard to dislike him and remember just how much pain he had once brought into her life.

'Lauren, you were too young. Foremost, you were my student and my first responsibility was getting you through those finals. The way we were going, it just wasn't going to happen.'

She laughed bitterly, the sound cracking with the embers of the fire. 'Wasn't it a bit too late to start thinking about that after what we had done?'

He looked down at his hands as he clenched them suddenly in his lap. 'You have every right to say that. And, God knows, I paid the price.'

'*You* paid the price?' she burst out, shaking with anger. 'Do you realise what you did to me when you told me I wasn't cut out for surgery?'

He jerked up his head, staring at her with a deep frown. 'What did you want me to do at the end of your training—lie to you? I could have, except you would have found out the hard way and batted your head against a brick wall for the next ten years, maybe all your life—'

'That was my decision to make—not yours!' she cut in, gripping the arms of the settee.

He shook his head wearily. 'Lauren, every doctor has a niche and surgery wasn't yours. You got too involved. You didn't think like a surgeon. You cared for your patients too deeply in a personal sense.'

'And what's so wrong with that?' she demanded. 'Is that a crime?'

'No, not a crime. But surgery is an attitude of mind, not just a skill. You didn't have it. Your talents lay in other directions. You did well as a house physician, didn't you? God knows why you gave it up.'

How could she tell him the truth? That her life had seemed meaningless without him and that she'd just had to get away from London, and she'd decided that if it meant she had to go to the ends of the earth in order to forget him then she would have to do it.

'That's beside the point,' she breathed, and sank back in her chair. 'My first concern now is the practice. This was my mother's life's work and now it is mine. I'm not giving it up and I'm not open to discussion on giving it up.'

'And I'm not asking you to,' he said, frowning at her. 'Look, after you left for Africa, your mother came to see me. She had been thinking of developing the practice for some time. She wanted to provide Gorsehall with the best possible healthcare she could in what was then a basically ill-equipped and overworked practice. To do this properly, she realised she would need to take on another partner and reinvest. She asked if I would consider buying into the partnership and eventually. . .I agreed.'

'But why you? She could have had her pick of any doctor.'

He averted his face, a tiny muscle working at the base of his jaw. 'She said because the Forest needed new blood, new energy and someone who was familiar with the latest technology. She knew me well enough through you. She felt. . .safer in asking me than a complete stranger.'

Lauren leant her head against the cool leather. Safer. That was a joke. Oh, why hadn't she told her mother about their break-up, the true reasons for it? That he had callously put an end to all her hopes and then finished with her, breaking her heart as though it had been some disposable item that could just be tossed away in a bin and forgotten about—

'You were gone, Lauren, remember?' His deep voice broke in sharply. 'Susan always hoped you'd show an interest, but—'

'She could still have asked me.'

He shrugged. 'She was a proud woman.'

'And so she asked you—of all people.'

'I only meant to stay at Gorsehall temporarily. But the practice extension was in the process of being built; there was so much to concentrate on. Planning permission, new equipment, an increase in catchment area. . .'

'But that doesn't explain why my mother sold you the house.'

He looked at her for a long time before replying. 'Hasn't it occurred to you that there might be a simple answer, like Susan wanting a smaller place—a flat or a bungalow which would suit her needs? That a rambling old house like this for one person was becoming too much? She wasn't in the best of health and she was becoming tired very easily—'

'You're saying. . .she was ill?'

'Her angina was troublesome. Not that that in itself was remarkable, but she was under a lot of pressure and she wanted to devote her time and energies totally to the practice.'

'And you just happened to be looking for a house?' she suggested, unable to hide the note of derision in her voice.

He paused, then said slowly, 'The truth is, I bought Gorsehall because your mother suggested it and although I would have in fact preferred to move out of the village altogether; she was very persuasive.'

'I don't believe you,' Lauren said flatly. 'She loved this house. It was where all her memories were. She would have wanted—' She stopped, unable to articulate her thoughts. She couldn't believe he had been acquiescent to her mother's wishes—more likely he would have seen an opportunity and used it.

'Let's face it—neither of us will ever know what she really had in mind,' he said on a deep sigh. 'But surely what we have to do now is reach some decision on the practice? We both know it needs commitment, and it needs it now.'

Lauren swung her legs from the settee, clutching the blanket. 'And what do you suggest?'

'I suggest we both give it our best shot. Because when Hugo goes—'

'What on earth do you mean?' Lauren gasped as she stared at him.

'He's had enough, Lauren. He's fifty-nine. Two years older than your mother when she died. Things have changed whilst you've been away. General practice has been transformed. The pace is faster; the whole concept of general practice is different. Hugo's one of the old school—one reason why your mother came to me in London. Hospitals have had to improve or close down. It's the same here. We have to aim for rapid and accurate diagnosis and offer patient care to the hospitals who can provide the swiftest services.'

Lauren wondered when and how Hugo had come to this decision. Despite all the changes in the health service, she was surprised that he was ready to go. Might not Eliot have encouraged the idea in more ways than one?

'You are certain about Hugo?' she asked doubtfully.

He shrugged. 'As certain as I can be.' He was stroking his chin with his hand and watching her carefully. 'But I do have a suggestion.'

She flicked up her gaze and her mouth twisted into a cynical smile. 'Oh, I'm sure you have.'

He ignored her. 'I'm suggesting we give the practice six months of our working together. You'll find out what's been happening in the health service and I'll find a locum to replace Hugo when and if he decides to go. We'll make full use of all of our new technology and make this place what your mother wanted. . .a successful and thriving surgery.'

'And if it doesn't work?' she thrust at him.

'We'll cross that bridge when we come to it. No strings. Just you and I on a professional basis, facing the challenge for the next six months.'

Put this way, she was forced to agree, it was at least giving the practice a chance. As her gaze met Eliot's she realised she really had no choice.

For the moment, there seemed no other way.

CHAPTER THREE

THE oddest thing was that waking up to the sounds of Eliot whistling in the kitchen below didn't seem in the least bit strange. She blinked at the dim light filtering in through the windows and heard his footfall on the stairs, turning her head sharply to see by the clock that it was almost six-thirty.

She pushed back her dark hair and sat up, stretching just as Eliot opened the door to stride across the floor and set a breakfast tray on the table beside her bed. He drew the curtains and pre-dawn light bathed the room. He wore his thigh-length black towelling robe, revealing strong brown calves which tapered down to large, well-formed feet attired in leather flip-flops. He moved as he had always moved—slowly, surely, in perfect control. She shivered and turned her attention to the tray, tugging the duvet up under her chin.

'Coffee and croissants,' he drawled. 'There's more downstairs.'

Slowly she emerged, sipped the delicious black liquid and found that it instantly revived her.

'We'll leave at eight,' he told her briskly, glancing at his watch. 'Surgery begins at eight-thirty. I'll introduce you to the reception staff first and then our practice nurse. We share her with the next village. All three come in on a part-time basis.'

She nodded, remembering her initial shock at his proposal last night. They both knew, though, after the challenge he had issued, that she would stay. Besides, at the end of six months she might have discovered a way to resolve her problems, the worst being the man

36

who now left her bedroom to go, whistling, down the stairs.

After drinking the coffee and showering, she coiled her hair into a shining pleat at the back of her head. Then she put on her favourite dark grey suit, which enveloped her warmly but softened the businesslike air it had with the excellent feminine cut to her slim waist and hips. Even though she had lost weight it fitted, since when she had bought it, it had been a size too small. Now it was perfect.

Going downstairs, she made her way into the garden through the French windows and breathed in the crisp October morning and the scents of the green garden. So similar to the heavy moistness of Africa in the rain. She closed her eyes, only to open them in a flash as she heard a movement and Eliot appeared beside her.

He was wearing an immaculate dark suit and tie, his dark hair brushed back, revealing the chiselled lines of his face, older now at thirty-four, but. . .and her heart almost stopped at the thought. . .more sensual, more sure, a man in perfect command of himself.

'You look better—are you?'

She nodded. 'Yes, I am, thanks.'

His eyes drifted admiringly over the soft femininity of the suit, slipping down to the extent of her long legs encased in stockings and high heels. She loved feminine clothes and had a wardrobe full of classical lines which were timeless. She felt good in chic attire—it even felt like armour at the moment against his gaze, and, heaven alone knew, she needed that.

'Do you want to take the Saab or come with me?'

'I'll take the Saab.'

He handed her the keys and lifted the double doors of the garage where the two cars were parked.

As they went to unlock, he called softly to her across the roofs of the cars. 'Lauren?'

She looked up, her uncertain green eyes widening.

'Thanks.' He smiled softly. 'I mean it.'

She hesitated, locked for a moment in time as she drifted back years. Then she stiffened, glanced sharply down and opened the Saab. As she started the engine, she realised she was trembling. . .and she continued to tremble all the way to the surgery.

The initiation was painless.

The two reception staff, Jessie Dunn and Robin Ward, both in their early thirties, were friendly and helpful, replacing her mother's elderly secretary who had long since retired and who had been her mother's only assistant. The practice nurse, June Whitham, was equally welcoming and refreshingly enthusiastic. There was one more member of staff, whom Eliot had forgotten to mention—Jane Garner, a capable, bespectacled lady, the practice manager.

Hugo came in and wrapped his big arms around her and, swallowing the lump in her throat, she could see just how right Eliot had been. Hugo had a grey head of hair now, instead of his once rich brown thatch. His face was lined and tired, but he still had his wonderful smile.

'We'll talk soon,' he whispered in her ear. 'Good to have you aboard.'

She nodded, wordless. Hugo was a reminder of her mother. It was both painful and yet reassuring. She took a breath and smiled as he hurried off to surgery.

'Sit in with me if you like,' Eliot suggested. 'Or I'll have the girls filter off patients to you, if you like?'

Lauren hesitated. She'd been far removed from this sort of work for two years; was she capable of taking surgery immediately? 'I'll sit in, if you don't mind, just for today.'

He nodded. 'Whatever you like.'

Eliot's room, like the other three consulting rooms,

were all white, bright and freshly decorated. Luckily the expedition with George Viner had made her familiar with the general run of the place. But watching Eliot in action was something else. She had forgotten just how good he was.

His patients were a mixed bunch, not many of whom she recognised: village people, commuters to the city and rural housewives and their families. Eliot treated them all with the same friendly but efficient attitude, just like the one he had displayed at the central London hospital when he had taught his students. One could have mistaken his attitude for brusqueness, but, underlying it, there was a distinct compassion which Lauren felt hard put to equate with her own experience of him.

During the morning, she began to wonder what had attracted him to general practice. She had been so sure that he was committed to a consultancy and that he loved the bustling hospital life—after all, hadn't they been wrapped up in it totally when they had first met?

She gave a little start as the last patient left, bringing her mind back to the present.

'Any questions?' He was staring at her with intent blue eyes, folding away the last of the documents and adding the information to his computer.

'I was interested in the young man's case—Lec Darby wasn't it?'

Eliot nodded. 'Real name David Smith. Base guitarist in a pop group. Epilepsy.'

Lauren frowned. 'Surely his work isn't conducive to helping his disease?'

Eliot smiled ruefully. 'Tell David that. He's pretty blasé about it. He says if he has a fit when he's playing no one will notice anyway—it's hard rock.'

She smiled. 'And he hasn't to date?'

'No. . .he collapsed backstage on tour last year. It wasn't a grand mal and he didn't fit for very long. He had another one and came to me six months ago. I sent him for an EEG, blood tests and CAT scan.' Eliot shrugged, leaning forward. 'Do you know that epilepsy is ten times more common than MS, yet for every pound we spend on epilepsy research, we spend a hundred and forty pounds on MS. Crazy, isn't it?'

She sighed and nodded. 'He's on medication?'

'Oh, we've tried several types of anticonvulsant. Whether he takes them or not is another matter. Today he came in for a repeat prescription, so I gather he is.' Eliot glanced at his watch. 'We'll get two or three visits in before lunch at this rate. Not hungry yet, are you?'

'No. . .no.' Lauren stood up, realising he was merely being polite in asking. After checking out with Reception and chatting to the girls briefly, he sped her off in the Rover and completed four flying visits before one-thirty. Then they ate a sandwich in the office, drank two huge mugs of coffee and shared a surgery from two until five. When this was over they flew through five more visits and then arrived back at Gorsehall, where he was on call for the night.

Lauren fell limply into a chair in the lounge, realising she had gone past hunger as he brought in a tray stacked with goodies. 'Sorry, but I haven't shopped recently. Will this do?'

She sat up, stretching her tired back, eyeing the assortment suspiciously. There was a rather extraordinary-looking cold ham, pickle, some flaky cheese, a hardish looking loaf, and butter which had seen better days. 'Is any of it edible?'

His smile was wry. 'Absolutely. Plenty of good, wholesome penicillin.' Then he attacked the pickle, piled it on the cheese and ate as if there were no tomorrow.

A small smile crossed her lips. She watched him gulp it down as she picked at her own food. Is this how he lived, she wondered curiously? Going from one day to another in a whirlwind of activity? Then hard on the heels of this thought came another. They had not discussed accommodation! Obviously she could not remain at Gorsehall. Just as she was about to bring up the question, the phone shrieked.

Jumping up from his meal, he leapt for the extension in the hall and seconds later he poked his head around the door. 'I'll have to take a rain check on the pudding.' He grinned. 'I've a young seventeen-year-old in the village who is presenting severe abdominal pain. It appears to have come on quite suddenly. Her mother describes the pain as discomfort around the navel, now localised in a small spot in the lower right abdomen. Apart from which, she's feverish and nauseated. . .et cetera.'

She sat up on the edge of her seat. 'Appendix?'

'Could be. I'll drive over straight away.'

'What about the phone? Do you want me to take calls?'

'Great. Ring me on the mobile if it's an emergency. Number's on the receiver.'

She nodded. 'OK. But what if—?'

The crash of the front door and roar of his engine told her not to bother and she sank back, feeling breathless herself. She stared at the half-eaten meal. Did this happen often? she wondered.

She closed her eyes, too tired to think. Soon she fell deeply asleep and did not hear a thing until he woke her.

'Come on, sleepyhead—bed!'

'You're back?' She sat up with a jolt. 'Was it an appendix?'

He nodded, pulling her to her feet. 'I admitted her straight away and they're doing an immediate appendectomy. None to soon either. The appendix had become so inflamed she yelled stars and stripes when I examined her.' He laughed softly. 'There's not a lot to be said

for those inconvenient little evolutionary relics is there?
Come on, don't go back to sleep.'

She followed him wearily up the stairs, conscious of
his large body filling her vision and the warmth of the
house closing around them.

He pushed open her door for her and grinned.
'Sleep well.'

She avoided the deep blue gaze and mumbled a
goodnight, dragging herself to the bed. The duvet
encompassed her as she expelled a soft, exhausted groan
and fell fast asleep.

If she had thought Monday was busy, by Friday she
had completely revised her opinion. The week had been
chaotic. Africa seemed an eternity away. She had begun
her own surgeries and with Hugo and Eliot's help had
managed to avoid any major problems. She learnt
quickly, getting to know her patients, and surprisingly
found the work incredibly satisfying. One elderly lady
was so taken with her that she asked for three visits and
named her specifically each time.

'How's it going?' Eliot met her in a brief lull late on
Friday afternoon.

She sighed. 'I think I've been on automatic pilot.
We've been so—'

'Frantic?'

She laughed softly. 'Understated!'

'Which is why I think we should advertise for that
locum right now before we get any busier.'

She nodded. 'Yes, I can see the need. And talking of
needs—I have to find somewhere else to stay,' she added
quickly, looking at him from under her lashes. 'I thought
I'd ask one of the girls if they know of any rented accommodation in the village.'

He stared at her in surprise. 'Bit drastic isn't it?'

'Well, obviously I can't remain at the cottage.'

'Why not?' His attention drifted as he checked his case and shrugged. 'Up to you, but I don't see the point of such an upheaval—as long as we steer clear of treading on one another's toes, of course.'

Lauren stood in silence and watched him go. Thoughtfully she slid on her coat and picked up her case wondering why she was even considering his last remark.

On Saturday, Lauren had a phone call from Tom Clancey who let her know that he had salvaged the hired car from Smithy's Ford, stored it in his workshops and was awaiting the rental firm's assessment. During the conversation he mentioned he'd been having a few dizzy spells and Lauren told him to come and see her in the surgery the following week.

Since she discovered they were low on supplies she made a trip into the village and stocked up herself. Eliot spent most of the day at the surgery and the evening too. He told her that what paperwork he didn't manage to do during the week he caught up on at the weekends, proving the point by disappearing all Sunday.

By the time Monday came around, Lauren was almost certain though, that he was deliberately keeping out of her way. In the morning before work, she heard his movements downstairs. After showering and dressing in a warm green cashmere sweater and pencil slim green skirt, she found her way to the kitchen and saw by the china washed up on the side, he had already breakfasted. She ate alone and glimpsed him briefly before he dashed off, fifteen minutes ahead of her.

Her morning surgery posed few problems, but in the afternoon she was surprised to see George Viner's wife walk in.

'Come in, Mrs Viner.' Robin had placed her files on the desk. 'How are your son and daughter?'

At Lauren's interest, she smiled faintly. 'Oh, not too bad. The boy's got a cast up to his thigh and Julie's ankle wasn't broken luckily.'

Lauren smiled and waited. 'So, how can I help?'

Shirley Viner pushed back her short dark hair, chewing on her lip. 'It's George, as a matter of fact. Something's. . .wrong. I don't know what. I can't really explain. He's. . .' She looked confused, searching for words. 'He's. . .behaving peculiarly. We've had terrible problems one way and another. The stables are only just keeping viable. Money has been short and George had been very worried. The past six months we haven't exactly been getting on very well.' She sighed, looking up at Lauren. 'Money problems do that, you know—drive you apart.'

Lauren frowned. 'You think he's depressed?'

'I just think everything's got on top of him. Maybe he's having a breakdown. This sounds ridiculous. . .but the other day there was one of the kid's bridles slung over the chair. He asked me whose it was. We must have had it for donkey's years. We had a terrible argument over it—so silly.'

'Does he complain of feeling ill? Headaches for instance?'

She nodded slowly. 'As a matter of fact he's gone through packets of paracetamol. Worry headaches I suppose.'

'Would he come to see me?'

She shook her head. 'You know George.'

'Well, all I can suggest is to try to persuade him. If there is something wrong, we should try to find out what it is as soon as possible. Come in together if it makes it any easier.'

The woman nodded and let out a doubtful sigh. 'Pigs might fly before George admits to being ill!'

Lauren felt sympathy for her as she watched her go,

a small figure in jodhpurs and waxed jacket. By the rounded slope of the woman's shoulders she had the impression that Shirley Viner was more worried than she cared to admit.

She had little time to consider this though, as Robin showed in her next patient, Polly Sharp, a thirty-five-year-old woman complaining of attacks of nausea and cramps. Lauren asked her to undress and gave her a full examination, isolating the main symptoms which seemed to be flatulence and sharp, abdominal discomfort.

Lauren read her notes, checking them on the computer. 'Well, I'm pretty certain you have irritable bowel syndrome,' she explained, glancing up at the attractive brunette. 'But to confirm it, I'd like an X-ray taken and possibly a barium meal.'

'Oh God, I don't much fancy that.' Polly Sharp pulled her expensive-looking fake fur coat around her and shuddered. 'And anyway, I work in London in PR. There's no one else who can really cover for me. I can't really afford to take time off. Couldn't you just give me something for the—what is it. . .?'

'Irritable bowel syndrome.' Lauren smiled patiently. 'I could, but I'd rather not until we've run the tests.'

Her patient sat forward. 'Listen, I'll think about it. Meanwhile, surely there's something I could have to ease the pain?'

Lauren was beginning to despair. Eliot had been right. Everyone seemed in a rush these days—health care seemed to be last on the list of priorities. 'Do you pay much attention to your diet?' Lauren asked deflectively.

Polly Sharp laughed. 'In my job? Heavens, the last thing I think about is what I eat. Why?'

'Because there are self-help measures I can recommend. . .aimed at restoring to normal the muscular contractions of the intestine.'

'Great! Let me have them and I'll be fine.'

Lauren smiled ruefully. 'We'll make a deal. I'll make you an appointment for diagnostic tests and I'll prescribe you some antispasmodic drug for the pain. Then I'd like you to come in to see me next week and we'll talk about self-help measures.'

'Next week? I'm on a course.' Her patient sighed doubtfully. 'Still, I might manage Friday.'

'Good. Get Robin or Jessie to make you an appointment.' Lauren wrote the prescription. However, she was still unhappy about Polly Sharp. Even if she did arrange tests, she could still see her cancelling—a problem she was thinking over later that evening when she arrived home and for once found Eliot there before her.

'Not eaten, I hope?' His greeting came as a surprise as she walked in. Delicious odours were coming from the kitchen. He was wearing a checked shirt and casual trousers and a tie-waist chef's apron, preparing what looked suspiciously like trout.

'No, I haven't as a matter of fact.'

'Good. I collected this from a local trout farm today. The guy who runs it is one of my patients. I tossed a couple of others in the freezer. See you've already done a bit of shopping yourself.' He glanced up, arching an eyebrow. 'Herbs?'

'What? Oh. . .er. . .yes.' She pulled off her coat, sniffing the assortment of vegetables bubbling on the hob. 'I wasn't aware you could cook.'

'I couldn't—once. But I've learnt.'

'Wonders will never cease,' she murmured and grinned as he caught her glance.

'You might well laugh,' he chuckled, 'but on occasion I've stuck my head in one of those cookery books of yours and tried a few experiments.'

Lauren sat down at the kitchen table. 'I don't think I've ever seen you boil so much as an egg.'

He straightened his back, finishing off his prep-
arations with a decisive snap of the knife. 'That's
because we never bothered much with food, did we?'

She hardly dared look at him for she knew what he
meant. Because time had been so precious, whenever
they had spent it together, they had never concerned
themselves with trivialities. And, over the weeks, eating,
studying and seeing other friends had for her come so
far down the list as to be called trivial, making her
ashamed to admit how little time she had devoted to
them. The only way she had managed to keep up with
her studies had been to cram when she could, even on
duty sometimes, and, as for meals, canteen sandwiches
and fruit had been her sole sustenance.

Guiltily, she remembered that on the few occasions
when Eliot had actually forced her to spend an evening
in and not at his flat she had been too distracted to
concentrate on her work for her finals. She had literally
begun to live only to see him, so obsessive had she
become in her feelings for him.

'Mint?' he asked her and she jerked up her gaze to
his eyes and saw in them the expression of intimacy that
made her feel he was reading every thought.

'Oh, yes, thanks,' she mumbled and watched him tear
a leaf from the little green plant that stood in a box in
the middle of the table.

She didn't try making eye contact again with him.
She didn't trust herself. Instead, she ate ravenously, finding the trout was so delicious that she was truly amazed
at how good it was. Afterwards they sifted out from the
freezer the ice cream she'd bought at the supermarket
and, when all the dishes were washed and put away they
sat with coffee by the fire.

'I'd like to visit Mother's grave tomorrow,' she told
him. 'It's something I should do.'

He nodded. 'I'll take you, if you like.' He bent

forward, long arms clad in a thick shirt, elbows resting on hard thighs, his gaze intent on her. 'I don't know if this helps, but she was very proud of you.'

Lauren sat back and closed her eyes. 'I just wish I'd known she wanted my help. I would have come home.'

They sat in a lingering silence, the sounds of the house—the old plumbing and the expansion and con-traction of the timbers in the heat—making her aware of how timeless the old place was. She knew every creak and groan and it seemed ever more impossible that this was no longer her home.

'I'd like to ask you a question,' he said as the last embers of the logs glistened in the grate. 'Something I've never understood. Why,' he said slowly, knitting his brows together, 'did you decide to go to Africa just when you were doing so well as a house physician?'

If he was trying to make her admit that it was because of their broken relationship and her inability to cope without him then he was going to be disappointed. She toyed with the idea of flatly refusing to answer for a moment and then decided that if it was an ego boost he was looking for then she would probably be playing into his hands either way. Finally she settled for half the truth.

'I wanted to do my bit, I suppose. The work interested me and I knew someone who had just come back from East Africa. She said the work was rewarding and that I would probably enjoy it.'

'And I suppose it didn't occur to you to say goodbye?'

'To you? Why should I? It wouldn't have meant anything.'

He looked at her for some time before he said, 'Because we had split up, it didn't mean that I didn't still care for you and care about you. . .what you did. . .where you went.'

Her mouth fell open. 'Do you seriously expect me to believe that?'

'Lauren, I know it looked pretty pathetic—'

She nearly choked. 'My God, Eliot, what did you think you were playing at? You couldn't even lend me a shoulder to cry on; you were so bored with our relationship—our *affair*. . .' she corrected herself scathingly. . . 'that you couldn't even wait until I'd qualified to finish with me.'

He shook his head, staring at her, a frown deeply etched across his brow, his lips moving as she rose to her feet. 'Lauren, listen to me. . .'

'I think we've just about exhausted the past,' she said as she wrapped her arms around herself and sighed. 'I'm tired, Eliot. I'm going to bed. Goodnight.'

She turned, walking wearily from the room, asking herself what the point was in allowing herself to be drawn by him. But as she reached the door strong fingers curled around her arm and stopped her, swinging her around to face him. 'Lauren, I never meant to hurt you. I thought it was best for you that I let you get on with your life.'

She was too full of emotion to speak. And then, quite suddenly, all the anger seemed to drain out of her as she stared into his eyes, leaving her trembling and vulnerable as his body brushed against her, sending little currents of sensations wildly galloping through her bloodstream.

'Oh, Lauren, I know I must have seemed like one hell of a bastard. . .'

She nodded, the tears welling up. All she could see was a blur.

'Oh, my darling. . .' His lips came down, slowly, gently, kissing away her tears. 'If I thought. . .' Then he stopped as they stared at one another, her tears drying saltily on her cheeks as she could hardly believe that the old chemistry was there, so powerful, rocketing through her body like a Roman candle splaying out its little lights to her fingertips and toes and making her feel alive for the first time in years.

She struggled weakly, telling herself this couldn't be happening again—it couldn't. All her instincts clamoured at the danger signals and yet, as his eyes flared, she was drawn inextricably into their power.

'Lauren, I have to explain. . .'

'It's too late for explanations, Eliot.'

'Do you really believe that?'

Her head swam. She bit down on her lip so that she could feel the pain and wake herself up from the dream. 'Please. . .let me go.'

Before she had time to say any more he was kissing her, his tongue sweetly probing open her lips, seeking out the response he knew was there, making her body come alive with the fire she remembered so well.

How could she stop herself? She wanted him—yet she hated him. Instead her mouth opened in surrender, her lips smouldering beneath his kiss as her hands slowly crept around his strong neck, her body relaxing into him, throbbing with the intensity of her need.

'Oh, God, Lauren, I've ached for so long for you,' she heard him whisper, and in that moment she almost believed him.

Lost to reason, she kept her eyes closed, drowning, escaping into the dream that had come alive, until suddenly she registered his persuasive movement, the slow drawing of her into the hall and towards the stairs. It was then she came awake, something in the cold calculation of his leading her upstairs making her realise what she was doing.

'You are a bastard!' she gasped. And then she pushed him away from her, her feelings in turmoil as one part of her so dearly wanted to be loved by him and to feel the excitement and joy that only he could bring. Yet the other part of her remembered the pain of four years ago—the pain that had once torn her life to shreds.

CHAPTER FOUR

THE aroma of breakfast coffee filled the house as Lauren came downstairs. In the second she had pushed him away last night she had felt a short-lived satisfaction as he had stared back at her, the expression in his deep blue eyes revealing his surprise.

She entered the kitchen and he looked up from pouring the steaming black liquid into cups, but the cool blue gaze showed nothing of the expression she remembered as she'd left him and hurried to her bedroom.

'Coffee?' He lifted the pot, but she was already shaking her head.

'I'm moving out today,' she said tightly, ignoring the offer.

'Because of last night?'

'Of course,' she returned sharply. 'You seem to think we can just pick up where we left off four years ago. That's why you suggested I stay, isn't it?'

'No. . .no, it wasn't, as a matter of fact.'

'And you expect me to believe you?'

'You're in no danger here, I promise,' he told her softly, returning to the task of filling the cups and handing her one. 'I didn't realise one little kiss would upset you so much.'

She gasped. 'One little kiss—'

'Well, maybe two,' he interrupted with a wry grin. 'Lauren, I kissed you. . .end of story—it wasn't a drama until you made one out of it.'

'A drama,' she repeated, gazing at him incredulously.

'Are you telling me I imagined that little scene of seduction?'

He raised a dark eyebrow, looking sickeningly handsome in an elegant charcoal-grey suit and tie, his black hair smoothed damply from his face after a shower. 'Look, you're making a mountain out of a molehill. Neither of us would have let it go further.'

'Eliot, you know that's not true.'

'For my part—it is. Though I'm not sure about you.'

She felt her jaw fall open, realising she had fallen into the trap, and she coloured, trying to think of something to say, but she was too confused to reason out a decent answer and just stood there instead, feeling an utter fool.

'Perhaps it was bound to happen,' he added calmly, taking pity on her. 'And, now that it has, we can both get on with the task in hand—which is concentrating on the practice, knowing exactly where we stand with one another.'

She managed to take a breath with lungs which felt as if they had been squashed by a steamroller. 'I knew where we stood before you made a pass,' she muttered, and took a sip of her coffee to camouflage her humiliation.

'Perhaps you needed me to make it? You certainly didn't put up much of a struggle. Perhaps rejecting me appealed to your sense of wounded pride?' he suggested with painful accuracy. 'And now that you've settled the old score perhaps we can begin to get on with our lives.' He walked past her, slid his cup back into its saucer on the table and picked up his case. 'See you at surgery.'

In shock she watched his broad-shouldered swagger as he walked away, the soft slam of the front door scraping at her nerve-ends. She was simply unable to believe how he'd turned that situation around the way he had, but then she'd rather asked for it, hadn't she? Her best plan would have been to come downstairs as if nothing had happened and then move her things out of the house when she was alone.

Now that was impossible because it would only prove him right. Whether she liked it or not she would have to stay and grit her teeth and bear it.

She sank down onto a stool and buried her face in her hands. She was sure she had interpreted his pass last night for what it had been—purely sexual interest, which would almost certainly have developed if she'd let it. She was the one who had stopped it, not him, as he'd suggested.

Well, he'd bitten off just a little more than he could chew this time. She would play him at his own game.

After the miserable beginning to the week, she managed to brazen out the rest—she had to because she needed to seek either his or Hugo's advice with regard to her patients.

She did, however, refuse his offer to take her to the cemetery and went alone. She left a posy of flowers there—small, unfurled roses and fern. She stayed a little while, allowing herself a few thoughtful moments, and she felt better once she had done that, knowing her mother would have been the last person to have wanted her to indulge in regrets. She cleared the debris from the fresh green grass and made a mental note to contact a stonemason.

The visit to the church seemed to mark a change in her life, for after this she felt more focused and able to deal with patients, who invariably wanted to talk about old times. She frequently recognised faces and began to realise how deep were her roots in the village. Ranging from six to sixty, people always had a memory they liked to share with her and as time went on Lauren welcomed the intimacy rather than avoiding it.

Surprisingly, Polly Sharp turned up on Friday, and

Lauren suggested she should keep a diary of her food and drink intake so that they might be able to identify particularly troublesome foods or liquids. She explained about a high fibre diet and its alternative, a bland diet, and tried to pin her patient down on her eating habits with very little success.

'But surely one is better than the other?' Polly asked in confusion.

Lauren paused. 'You'll probably need to experiment to find out which. I was hoping we might isolate some food which doesn't agree with you, but I think you're just going to have to put in a bit of time and patience as far as your eating habits go.'

Polly raised her eyes to the ceiling. 'That's all I need, with my schedule. Anything else?'

Lauren smiled ruefully. 'We need to think about the type of bowel motion—'

'Oh, charming!' Polly groaned, and both women laughed.

'And relative stress factors,' Lauren added firmly. 'Of which I should imagine there are plenty?'

'Oh, I could write a book on that subject,' Polly confirmed, and listed any number of suspect areas in her highly pressurised job.

'Well, try what we've discussed and come and see me after your tests,' Lauren said eventually. 'And make sure you go,' she threatened with a smile, wagging a finger.

When her consulting room was clear, she swivelled her chair to gaze from the window onto the dense green thickets of the New Forest. A few motley ponies stuck their heads over the practice's fence in hope of titbits and a tractor rolled by, its thick tyres spraying up mud. Two thatched roofs poked up from the greenery and a chimney curled smoke peacefully into the air. She could hear the murmur of patients' voices in Reception and even recognised one or two now.

There was a good feeling to general practice, she had to admit. Not the kind of reward she had received in dealing with her poverty-stricken patients in Africa or the challenge of Theatre which she had so much desired. . .but there was something else. . .something deeply satisfying.

As a girl, she had never been able to see the attraction of general practice. Perhaps it had been rather like living in a sweet shop, she thought suddenly. You got sick of eating so many candies. With her having two GPs as parents, her life had revolved totally around general practice and maybe, if she was honest, she'd got a little sick of it too. More so after her father had died in a car accident. She'd been six years old and she had so few personal memories of him.

With an effort, Lauren brought her mind back to the present and Tom Clancey, who turned out to be her next patient. His BP was high and he hadn't been taking his pills, by the look of his occasional repeat prescriptions. She recognised her mother's handwriting on his notes. 'You saw my mother regularly, Tom?'

He laughed shyly and pushed back a lock of grey hair from his temple. Lauren thought he must have been a handsome individual in his youth and his eyes were still a deep, sparkling brown. He sat forward and she almost thought he was blushing.

'As a matter of fact, I would have seen her a lot more if she'd let me.'

She frowned. 'I'm sorry?'

He hesitated and then said quietly, 'I was crackers about her. We'd known each other for so long; we were good friends. But for me it grew to be more than that over the years. I'd have married her like a shot if she'd have had me.'

Lauren sat back in her chair, utterly surprised. Tom

Clancey had always been around—she'd known him as a child—the village wonder-worker who owned the garage and petrol station and performed all sorts of DIY miracles. He was part of village life—a bachelor of renown. She had no idea he'd been seeing her mother.

'Oh, don't worry, lass,' he chuckled. 'She wouldn't have married again. This place was the big love of her life after your father went.' The soft smile died and Lauren could see he had cared deeply. 'We were good friends and that meant a lot to me. I just wished she'd confided in me a bit more. But she wasn't like that. Very private lady, she was, right up to the end.'

Lauren nodded slowly, feeling a surprising measure of relief mixed with the shock of Tom's amazing revelation. There had been someone else who'd loved her mother too—and who had wanted to help.

Because Eliot was on call the following week and she the one after that, it meant that November arrived in what seemed like the bat of an eyelid. An uneasy truce developed between them as the flow of winter flu injections and viral complaints became all consuming, and her move from Gorsehall was not referred to again.

They had advertised for and taken on a locum. Charles Lee was a bright young man of thirty and he was looking for a permanent partnership in the Forest, though he'd eagerly accepted the temporary vacancy when it had been offered. Lauren had liked him immediately at interview and Hugo had found no fault either.

On her birthday on the second, the staff organised a small party after surgery. To her surprise, everyone brought her a small gift. Eliot arranged for a bouquet to be delivered—a tasteful selection of winter blossoms and gypsophila. Jessie and Robin and the practice nurse presented her with coffee-coloured silk underwear, the practice manager, Jane, had chosen a rather workmanlike but expensive pen and Biro set and Hugo and Charles had bribed one of the girls to buy for them a pale green silk blouse, the colour of her eyes exactly.

She had just turned her attention to Charles when, slightly emboldened, he slipped his hand around her waist and brushed her cheek with a kiss.

Lauren joked it off and to her surprise responded for a few seconds by way of a deep blush. It wasn't until she felt a laser burning through her shoulderblades that she turned to discover Eliot staring at her, his eyes levelled over Jane Garner's tweed-coated shoulder.

'If I'd known what general practice was like in the depths of the New Forest I would have applied before,' laughed Charles in his friendly manner. 'Happy birthday, Lauren.'

She blushed again, staring up into his eyes, which she suddenly realised were trained on her in a very appreciative way. 'Thank you, Charles. I hope you'll be very happy here. And thank you for the lovely blouse.'

He laughed softly. 'Hugo and I cheated. Robbie's taste, I'm afraid. But I have to say it does match those lovely green eyes of yours.'

Lauren was thankful when Jessie came over and offered the plate of canapés. Why, she wondered, was she responding like a sixteen-year-old to Charles's flattery? Possibly because for two years she hadn't had the opportunity to interact socially, she decided. Africa had been an all-or-nothing commitment and then the malaria had made her feel so very shabby—so why shouldn't she blush a little when a handsome young man paid her attention?

'Enjoying yourself?'

Lauren turned and gazed up into the deepest of blue eyes. Funny how the depth of them changed. . .the way they suddenly lit up in a silvery light and then melted to a deep, deep blue. . .

'Yes, I am, as a matter of fact.' She nodded to the vase she had placed on the shelf, overflowing with huge lemony white blooms. 'Thank you for the bouquet. The flowers are beautiful.'

His gaze rested only briefly on them and moved swiftly across to Charles who was regaling the girls with his jokes.

'He has quite the bedside manner.'

'Yes; refreshing, isn't it? I like him.'

The blue gaze whipped back. 'That's obvious.'

She felt hot colour flush her cheeks. 'And what's that supposed to mean?'

He arched a crooked brow. 'You tell me.' Before she could catch her breath she was stopped from answering as he added sharply, 'Anyway. . .I just came over to wish you a happy birthday. Twenty-seven. . .? Tell me. . .do you remember your twenty-second by any chance?'

Lauren felt herself tense. 'No, not particularly,' she lied and looked away. But she knew she hadn't fooled him. She would, as it happened, never forget her twenty-second birthday. The hospital had put on a crazy do in the refectory. Everyone had been there. She had had the world at her feet—she'd thought—a promising career ahead of her in surgery and a man with whom she had fallen passionately in love, despite knowing better, despite all the warnings in the world.

It had been the night of that party when they'd first made love. They had slipped away from the celebrations quietly without being seen and gone back to his flat. He'd been gentle and loving—and utterly shocked. She would never forget it, the sudden realisation in his eyes that she had given him her virginity, and he'd hugged her to him, imagining that she had been afraid. . .when her body had been intoxicated, satiated and trembling with pleasure.

'Lauren! Happy birthday, my dear girl!' Hugo caught her in a bear hug and the spell was broken. Eliot moved away, dragging his gaze from her face, and she pretended to concentrate on Hugo and his retirement plans.

With one ear she listened to Hugo—a cruise first with Amy, his wife, then seeing more of the grandchildren and breezing off to friends and family he hadn't seen for years. But she covertly watched Eliot drift away, talk, laugh, joke, turn his face in that special way, smiling that special smile at the girls.

Suddenly she felt very tired. She felt she had come such a long way since that hospital party and yet. . .nothing had really changed. He still devastated her. He still made her feel this way.

Damn him.

And what made her feel worse, though she would have died rather than admit it, was the arrival of a very attractive young woman at the house, two days later.

'Hello. You must be Lauren?'

Lauren was just preparing herself supper. Eliot was out on call and she was making the most of having the kitchen to herself. After the trout they had shared together and the subsequent quarrel, she had been careful to avoid clashing with him, an easy manoeuvre since the on-call rota had kept either one or the other of them away from the house, and by fair means or foul they had avoided one another.

Lauren frowned, smiling curiously as they stood at the front door. 'I'm sorry? Are you a friend of my mother's?'

The girl shook her fair head. 'No,' she answered hesitantly. 'Of Eliot's actually. I was supposed to meet him here at eight.'

Lauren paused, suddenly aware of the yawning gap in her knowledge of Eliot's personal life. Why had she imagined he hadn't any, for a start? Perhaps because they'd been so busy—and perhaps because she hadn't wanted to think about it. Guiltily, she glanced at the pretty girl and tried to look welcoming. 'Would you like to wait? He should be home soon.'

'Well. . .if it's not too much trouble.'

Caroline Peters, Lauren discovered, was a young woman with whom Eliot had become friendly during the summer. Lauren tried to guess her age, whilst telling herself she wasn't at all interested. But the large hazel eyes and short, bobbed fair hair which surrounded Caroline's young and intelligent face invited Lauren to make several private guesses, the best of which she fancied to be twenty-one at most.

'You're in advertising? What sort?' Lauren asked as they walked into the kitchen.

'Medical, as a matter of fact. Which is how I met Eliot. I work for a pharmaceutical company. They approached a number of doctors whom they asked for help with research on a new product.'

Lauren smiled. 'How interesting.'

Caroline nodded enthusiastically. 'He's really been most helpful. He's so. . .understanding, so easy to talk to.'

Lauren gritted her teeth and tried harder to smile.

Caroline tilted her head and blinked her long lashes. 'Eliot told me you've worked in Africa. How exciting. I've always wanted to travel.'

So, Eliot had been discussing her, had he? She could imagine what he'd said—and that Caroline was probably being polite in choosing Africa as the most innocuous subject she could refer to. As she floundered for an answer, the phone rang and she went gratefully to answer it. It was Hugo asking a favour. Shirley Viner had rung in a panic about George and needed a visit, but Hugo's grandson, who was staying with them, had fallen over and gashed a knee.

'I'll go,' Lauren offered immediately. 'Mrs Viner came in to see me after the accident and I would like to see her husband, as a matter of fact.'

'You're sure?' Hugo sounded relieved.

'Absolutely.'

'Thanks, Lauren. Tell Eliot he can leave the rest of the weekend to me.'

Lauren said she would convey the message and walked back into the kitchen, where Caroline had taken off her coat and was smoothing down a tight-fitting skirt over her feminine hips and very shapely thighs. The sudden sight of her making herself at home brought Lauren up sharp as she explained she had to go out.

'Oh, no problem.' Caroline smiled sweetly. 'I'm sure Eliot won't be long. Perhaps one evening we can make up a foursome for a meal? Eliot knows some wonderful watering holes in the Forest.'

Lauren stared at her, uncomprehending, for a moment. And then enlightenment dawned. She felt a sharp pain which she put down to the half-eaten supper she had discreetly pushed to one side.

Saying goodbye, she left, collecting her coat and case on the way out. In the bitingly cold air, she took a deep breath and steadied herself.

Caroline Peters had to be Eliot's girlfriend—idiot that she was, not to have realised immediately. It was the girl's youth that had confused her. Obviously he was going in for cradle-snatching these days. . .not that it should surprise her.

But it did.

And she was annoyed with herself. For did it matter a shred who his latest lover was? Not in the least, she told herself resolutely, and drove, tight-lipped, to Viner's Stables.

CHAPTER FIVE

SHIRLEY VINER drew the reins from the big strawberry roan's neck and handed them to one of the young stable lads whom Lauren remembered from the day of the accident. 'Thanks for coming,' she breathed on a deep sigh as she walked with Lauren to the house. 'I'd hoped it would be you. We had another little accident earlier.'

Lauren frowned. 'Not another pole?'

Shirley shook her head. 'Oh, no. Nothing so straight-forward unfortunately.' She gave Lauren a weary smile. 'It's George. This may seem ludicrous, but he went to mount a horse this morning—the first time since that day—and it was just as if he'd never ridden before. His footing was all wrong, he couldn't control his actions and the horse knew it. I had to lead the blessed animal back into the stables and George disappeared. In the end I sent the ride off with one of the girls.'

Lauren nodded thoughtfully. 'Have you noticed any other unusual behaviour?'

'All the time,' sighed Shirley bitterly. 'And we argue over it. John and Julie avoid him because he's so strange. He's getting more and more depressed. Now he's locked himself in the bedroom and he won't answer me. 'I'm really worried, Dr Kent.'

The house was a jumble of riding accoutrements and half of the dining room had been turned into a makeshift kitchen. John and Julie sat at the table doing their studies and Shirley led Lauren upstairs to the bedroom. Lauren tried to engage George's attention and for a while received no response from behind the locked door. Then she suggested Shirley make a cup of tea and, whilst she was away, asked George if he would like to talk about what was worrying him. The door slowly opened and a pale and worried man stood there, his hands hanging limply by his sides.

Lauren made no move to enter. 'May I come in, Mr Viner?'

George Viner shrugged and Lauren realised he was in a deep state of depression. She walked slowly in and closed the door behind her, sitting down in one of the two big armchairs which served as wardrobes to a chaotic pile of jodhpurs and waxed jackets.

After a while, he sat down too and Lauren heard the approach of Shirley outside. However, no knock came and she was grateful to be left alone with her patient. George slowly began to tell her of the confusion and bewilderment he felt at his own behaviour. He couldn't ride. He couldn't remember people and names and very often in the middle of the night he'd wake up in a panic and not know where he was. Sometimes he was unsure where he was and what he was doing even in daylight. Once he had been unable to shovel manure into a barrow.

Lauren listened as she checked the small wound she had first noticed at the back of his head.

'I think I'm going mad,' he told her as she found the innocent-looking abrasion which had virtually healed. 'I'm terrified of doing anything in case I can't. Even little things like cleaning tack. I dread Shirley finding out. I forget so many things. I don't know what people must think of me. I feel so ashamed.'

'Well, you are definitely not going mad, Mr Viner,' Lauren said gently, and sat down again. 'But you are becoming depressed because of harbouring suspicions about your mental state. I think you are having blackouts and this may be the direct result of a biological disorder, not a psychological one.'

'You don't think the worry of the house and all is

getting on top of me? That I'm losing my grip?'

'I think you are extremely worried, yes. You've had a lot of stress lately—the house, the family, keeping your business going. But I also think we must eliminate any physical damage—from a fall, for instance—which might have caused injury or the loss of basic sensation. . .even impair mobility. I would like you to see a specialist, Mr Viner. I really must urge you to agree—I can't help you otherwise.'

The man obstinately shook his head. 'You mean a shrink?'

'No, not a psychiatrist—a neurologist. Someone who will be able to decide whether you have a biological problem.' She looked with sympathy at the crestfallen man and finally left him with a tentative agreement to do as she suggested, and she promised to arrange an appointment for him as soon as possible.

Shirley Viner remained unconvinced. They had been having problems from before the accident and she was inclined to believe her husband was 'cracking up'.

Lauren drove back to Gorsehall preoccupied. She had a hunch George Viner was simply not just depressed. She couldn't prove it, but she felt sure that the depression was a result of something more tangible than the worry he had been under.

As she drove up to Gorsehall Cottage, she remembered Caroline. There was no vehicle in the drive—though she hadn't noticed one as she'd left. Nor could she see the Rover, but that could be in the garage.

She pulled the car up directly outside. The house was flooded with light. If Caroline and Eliot were in—she would find some excuse to go out again. She swallowed, got out of the car and fiddled for her key in the bottom of her bag. The minute she stuck it into the lock, another thought came to her. What if they were upstairs, in the bedroom?

She froze then drew the key out again.

Idiot, she told herself as a cold tide of uncertainty spread over her and drained her cheeks. Did it matter? Did it concern her what they were doing—or even where they were doing it?

Hesitantly she returned the key to her bag. A light shone down from Eliot's room as she stumbled to the car and yanked open the door. She was freezing, tired, hungry and this was just too ridiculous for words!

'Going somewhere?'

She spun around, a cry gulped back as she nearly jumped out of her skin. Eliot was standing at the door. A tiny hand-towel covered his slim hips and the curious frown on his forehead was the extent of what else he wore.

She made some kind of noise. It sounded suspiciously like a feeble excuse that she'd forgotten her keys. The tall, brown, very wet body moved and glistened as he flicked on the downstairs light. 'Good thing I heard you. I had the shower going full pelt a few minutes ago.'

Somehow she managed to walk past him, averting her eyes, but whichever way she looked she saw some part of his anatomy; a broad and glistening hair-roughened chest, long brown legs covered in the same coils of black hair, and exceptional thighs, all rounded and honed muscle.

She jerked sharply to her left and walked towards the kitchen, fully expecting to see Caroline where she had left her. He ambled lazily after her and watched as she removed her coat and set down her case by the table. Her heart almost stopped. Two cups, milk and sugar.

'How was your call?'

She gazed blindly at them. 'What? Oh, you mean George Viner? He is very depressed, but I'm not sure it's psychological. In fact I feel sure it isn't.' She stopped, waiting for him to mention his visitor.

Instead there was silence and he moved towards her and reached out to lift a long strand of rich brown hair which prevented him from fully seeing her face— a movement which made her jerk her body in sudden alarm.

He sighed. 'Lauren, for God's sake, relax. Look, we live in the same house, eat from the same table, use the same shower—albeit at different times—yet you would think I was your worst enemy. I've told you you're safe here. I meant what I said.'

Her heart lurched. He was, of course, telling her the truth. Perhaps even at this moment Caroline lay upstairs, in between his sheets. This knowledge made no difference to the way her treacherous body trembled as water dripped from his arm and fell on her hand.

The telephone rang and with a muted curse he let her hair fall back across her cheek and walked away. She heard him take it in the hall. Panic engulfed her as she decided she must get to the safe harbour of her own room. She almost ran past him and up the stairs. At the top, the temptation to look along the hallway was irresistible. The door of the green room was wide open. Her heart somersaulted as she stared in. The bed was made. There were no bras or panties littered over the floor and no trace or scent of a woman. She closed her eyes in relief and held onto the banister. Guiltily she flicked them open as she heard the phone go down.

'Just Tom Clancey to say your hire car has been collected by transporter and is on its way back to the leasing company.'

'Oh. . .thanks.' Her voice was shaky as she looked over the banister. 'Did you find your visitor when you came home?'

A very small, insignificant pause. 'Caroline? Yes, I did.'

Lauren waited, but as he obviously wasn't going to

elaborate she called swiftly, 'Goodnight, Eliot,' and went to her room, flicked on the light and breathed deeply as she gently closed the door.

She hated herself for being so curious. By rights she shouldn't give a damn about Caroline Peters.

Lauren stared at the pale face in her mirror, and at the almond-shaped green eyes that revealed the plain truth of her curiosity. She only prayed that Eliot had been unable to read them.

The aftermath of October's storm had left many of those who lived in the Dip near Smithey's Ford with ruined lower floors. With the quick return to normal working life, the small community of fifteen to twenty cottages in the road had been forced to abandon mucky carpets and water-soaked upholstery. With the evacuation of damaged goods came a further sweep of viral complaints and it was as Lauren was on her way to one of these that she crossed Smithey's Ford for the first time since her accident.

She had cold shivers driving over the small bridge and avoided looking down into the tiny, harmless-looking stream, no longer swollen. Only when she was over the other side and parked along her patient's drive did she turn to look back. The sensation of the water creeping up her legs came back. If Eliot hadn't been there to pull her out, would she have got free? Tom Clancey had arrived on the scene, but would he have been too late?

Lauren realised then that she had never really thanked Eliot for saving her life. The shock of what she'd found at Gorsehall had wiped all thought of thanks from her mind. But now, on this wonderful November day when glorious sunshine melted its way through the barren trees and the breath from her mouth lingered in the air, she had pangs of guilt—guilt which soon deepened when her housebound patient told her how she had first met Eliot Powers in the village shop a year ago.

'Reading out his list, he was, trying to make chicken broth and egg custard.' Ellen Smith sat up in her bed, nursing a temperature. 'Looked after your mother like she was his own,' Ellen sighed. ''Course, we were all a bit anti him when he first came—new ideas and so on, changing the surgery around. But my Pauline got tested with that ultrasound machine. She had an ovarian problem and Dr Powers discovered it and she got taken in straight away. Fit as a fiddle, she is now.'

Lauren listened patiently, curious despite her search in trying to diagnose a problem beneath her stethoscope. 'Well, Mrs Smith,' she sighed eventually, 'as far as I can tell it seems like a bout of gastroenteritis—'

'We've all had it along here. It was the flood, you know.'

'Yes, so I believe.' Lauren sighed sympathetically. 'Did you lose much?'

'Carpets and furniture—and David's guitar. Still, it was on the insurance. Just the trouble of finding another to replace it. It was his lucky one.'

'David?' Lauren hesitated as she packed her case.

'Lec Darby, he goes by on stage. He's my son. One of Dr Powers' patients too.'

Lauren smiled. 'Oh, yes. He's very dedicated, isn't he?'

The older woman sighed. 'That's putting it mildly. Potty about music, he is. Drove us mad as a youngster, wanting a guitar. All the other kids were pony-mad in this area. He taught himself, you know. He'd go a long way in the music business 'cept he's got himself in with a girl—eighteen, she is. Hardly more than a child herself.'

'Perhaps a girlfriend would help him keep his feet on the ground,' Lauren ventured mildly.

'Humph!' Ellen Smith was not impressed. 'My

David's a free spirit. Doesn't need no tying down, not with his talents.'

Lauren managed to change the subject and repeated her advice to drink plenty of fluids and to eat a light diet the following day until the blood chemistry was balanced again. Having explained that antibiotics and painkillers would only serve to aggravate the condition and possibly worsen the diarrhoea, she left Ellen Smith and made her way back to the surgery, feeling a little less wary on her second time across the ford.

When she arrived back, Eliot was with June Whitham, the practice nurse, in the ultrasound clinic.

'Coming in?' June called, poking her head around the door of the clinical investigations room.

Lauren nodded enthusiastically and spent the next hour with Eliot and June and several pregnant mothers gazing at the miracles which were becoming apparent within the safe walls of body tissue, as sound waves recorded the picture of each unborn child onto the screen.

After the clinic, Eliot washed up beside Lauren. 'I'll leave you to next week's clinic if you like,' he said, and gave her a wry smile. 'You seemed to enjoy yourself in there.'

'Who wouldn't? All babies doing well. No abnormalities and several very happy mothers.' She smiled. 'Thanks, I'd like to take the clinic.'

He nodded. 'The ultrasound was our first big invest-ment, for obvious reasons. Last week I had a patient who required scanning of his abdominal cavity. I covered gall bladder, pancreas and kidneys and identified the problem all within an afternoon. We cut out the middle man—the hospital—saved time and money and, most of all, the patient was much happier. Same with the cryoprobe. We can use it on a wide range of skin conditions and dispense with unnecessary referrals—'

'Commonly used for the removal of cataracts and the

destruction of certain bone tumours,' she interrupted as he picked up the instrument to show her.

'You've got it in one. On-the-spot cryosurgery.' He grinned, pointing to the fine point of the cryoprobe. 'The tip is cooled by carbon dioxide or nitrous oxide gas and, low and behold, we have a little miracle right at our fingertips, whereas once upon a time the patient would have had to wait for an appointment and then get himself to the hospital for treatment.'

Lauren sighed. 'In Africa we were lucky to have sterile syringes.'

'Seems unfair, doesn't it?'

For a moment they stood in silence then June came bustling in with the list of next week's clinic.

'Well, we're all finished I think, June,' Eliot said with a smile. 'I'll leave you to it.'

'He's gorgeous, isn't he?' June whispered and giggled. 'I wouldn't mind practising my ultrasound on that abdomen!'

Both women burst into laughter and Lauren found herself still smiling as she left surgery. She realised afterwards, though, that she had shared the amusement so readily because June was a fifty-year-old, cuddly, bubbly married woman who posed no real threat.

Now what if it had been Caroline Peters who had said that?

'Dr Kent, it's Shirley Viner here.'

'Hello there. What can I do for you?'

'I'm not sure actually.' There was a small pause. 'George's appointment has come for that specialist you were talking about. Trouble is, it's not till after Christmas. And, to be frank, I'm getting desperate. I don't know how much more I can stand. He won't talk and he goes missing for ages. I'm out of my mind with worry.'

Lauren asked her for the appointment date and time and said she would investigate. It turned out when she rang the Hospital for Neurology and Neurosurgery that the consultant Mrs Viner had named was on leave and his secretary had made all non-urgent appointments for after Christmas. Lauren queried it, but was further frustrated by the inability to talk to anyone with authority to help her.

Just as she put the phone down, Eliot walked into the office. For a week they had moved politely around one another, separated luckily by the spate of viral complaints which had dogged the village and had kept them busy both day and night. Because this meant their paths had still not crossed at Gorsehall Cottage, the head-on collision over domestic arrangements that Lauren feared might happen had been narrowly avoided.

He was now looking uncertain, raising dark eyebrows as he poked his head around the door. 'Got a moment?'

She nodded. 'Yes, come in.'

He ruffled his dark hair with pensive fingers, a frown creasing his forehead. 'I've David Smith with me at the moment—Lec Darby to his fans? He's. . .ah, got himself into a spot of bother.'

'Did he fit on stage?'

'No. Quite another problem. He's put one of the village girls in the family way.'

'And they aren't ready to make a commitment?'

Eliot smiled ruefully. 'Well, she's eighteen and lives at home with Mum and Dad. David's always off on tour. Her family want her to have an abortion. She's pretty distraught.'

'And what is it you would like me to do?'

'Have a chat with her. David's sitting in there with her like a waxwork. He obviously is keeping stumm. I'd like to talk to him—'

'But you can't with her there?'

He nodded. 'Something like that.'

Lauren sighed. 'OK. Give me a moment to sort this out.' She shuffled George Viner's files together and was about to put them in the pile for Jessie to take out when Eliot stopped her.

'George Viner?' he asked, catching sight of the name.

She nodded, looking up. 'I'm sure it's something more than clinical depression. I was hoping Morris Leyton would have a look at him, but he's on leave.'

'Morris Leyton from St Margaret's?'

She nodded. 'I always thought he was a first-class neurologist. He's at the Central now and I was hoping to have a word with him but, as I said, he's on leave. They can't give an appointment till after the holiday and I. . .well, I have an uneasy feeling that's going to be too late.'

'Too late? You mean you think he's at risk in some way?'

She nodded. 'Gut instinct, maybe. I could be quite wrong. Maybe he is just fed up with his business going under and the house being wrecked.'

Eliot hesitated. 'Look, I'll have a chat to you later. I'd better get the girl in. Her name is Chrissie Searle and her family are on our books.'

Whilst she waited, Lauren flipped up Chrissie's records on the computer. The last time she had been seen was two years ago when she had been prescribed Amoxil for a mild infection.

Chrissie eventually sidled in, her New Age trinkets and sandals looking incongruous in the cold weather. The shawl she wore around her shoulders disguised the fact that she was slim, and her prettiness was hidden under a tangle of orange dreadlocks.

'Hello, Chrissie. I'm Lauren Kent.'

Chrissie sniffed and sat down, resolutely silent.

'Would you like to talk, Chrissie?'

'There's nothing to talk about,' the girl snapped.

'Not even about your baby?'

She looked terrified. 'They all want—' she blurted out, and bit down on her lip.

Lauren felt a strong surge of sympathy and smiled gently. 'Chrissie, it's what you feel that matters most. What do you want?'

She began to cry, wiping away the tears with the back of her hand. Lauren handed her a tissue. 'I. . .I don't know.'

'Then you must have time and space to think about it—and to talk to David. Don't be pressured by anyone. Just try to think what you really want, whether you think you can cope with a child and whether you feel able to give him—or her—all the love that's so important.'

Chrissie looked up tearfully. 'You mean you don't think I should have an abortion?'

'It isn't a question of what I think. . .or anyone else thinks. This is your life and you and David have created something between you which is very precious. Make the time and effort to talk to one another about it.'

'I want to,' she sobbed, her face crumpling. 'Me and David love each other. But my dad says the baby will have what David has. That it'll be funny in the head.'

Lauren felt a moment's surging fury and then realised that the myth and prejudice surrounding epilepsy was probably even more rampant in a small community than it had been in the wilds of Africa, where there too it had had its own sad connotations as a 'mad' disease.

'Chrissie, do you know what epilepsy is?' she asked gently.

Chrissie shrugged. 'Not really. But I've seen David have a fit. He kind of chews with his mouth—and jerks around. I thought he was messing about. . .and then he told me afterwards—about the fits.'

Lauren nodded. 'Well, then, you know the worst—

what it looks like. But you also know David isn't funny in the head. Fortunately epilepsy can usually be well controlled with drugs so that people with the disorder can lead normal lives.'

Chrissie listened intently and Lauren could tell she had been fed a great deal of rubbish regarding her boy-friend's condition. Still, she looked a bright girl and she was obviously thinking deeply about her unborn child.

'Look, perhaps this will help.' Lauren sorted out some booklets from her drawer. 'Here are the true facts and figures on epilepsy and some information on the little embryo growing inside you. Talk about it with David. Then come back and see me next week, will you?'

The girl hesitated, then stood up and Lauren thought she might well walk away ignoring the offered infor-mation. But to her surprise she took it and slid it into her pocket. Without turning back and without uttering a word, she left the room.

Lauren ran a hand over her eyes. Had she handled that properly? She would have liked to have talked— really talked with Chrissie, poor little soul. But it was a question of building up trust—and she couldn't do that in five minutes. Besides, it was really Eliot's case and she could only go so far.

Some time later he came in and eyed her speculatively. 'Well, what do you think?'

'Of Chrissie?' She shrugged. 'I think there's a lot of pressure on both of them. I saw David's mother recently and she disapproves of the girl, or, at least, of her son having any responsibilities other than his music. Chrissie's parents are equally opposed. What with his career and the epilepsy to contend with, it won't be easy.'

'But?' He waited, watching her.

'But I think she loves him.'

He gave a cynical laugh. 'Love? Will love rectify the situation? Will it make David approach his illness any more maturely, or deter her parents from persuading her he's a cretin? Or make his almost impossible lifestyle any easier to handle—on tour with a screaming baby? Or with Chrissie being left behind to brood in God knows where—a bedsit or squat or a converted bus?'

Lauren felt her cheeks flush deeply. 'Don't scorn love, Eliot. It might not be the cure-all that science is supposed to provide, but it can work miracles if it's nurtured and preserved.'

'Even under their circumstances?'

She lifted her chin. 'David and Chrissie don't know how fortunate they are.' Her green eyes glistened intently. 'I saw dispossessed families in Africa— families decimated by war and poverty and disease— still cling onto life, mothers for their babies' sakes, children for the old folk. They refused to die because they still loved and valued someone. And they didn't even have a tent to live in.'

Eliot was quiet, sinking down into the patient's chair. He looked up at her and quirked a cynical eyebrow. 'Love is it, which conquers all?'

'It might be, in David and Chrissie's case.'

'So you advised her against an abortion?'

'No, I did not. It wasn't up to me to advise anything.' She looked at him steadily. 'How was David?'

'Angry.'

'Because of the pregnancy?'

'No. Because of what her parents had called him. And, I suspect, the fact that he himself is still coming to terms with epilepsy and its repercussions.'

'Then maybe now he'll make an effort to help himself more.'

He shrugged. 'Maybe. Or perhaps he's in denial and refuses to accept it.'

Lauren sat back and chewed on her lip. There was little either of them could do, other than to be there to listen if and when David and Chrissie returned. The couple had to work it out for themselves and it was, to all intents and purposes, she admitted silently, a sad start to any relationship.

Eliot hauled himself up, thrusting a large hand through his dark hair. 'By the way, I rang Morris. Had a word in his ear about George Viner.'

'Morris Leyton?'

He nodded. 'We still keep in touch. He's an obsessive golfer. Used to drag me off at St Margaret's and hammer me occasionally on the greens.'

Lauren realised they must be about the same age— possibly Morris was a couple of years older—but she hadn't realised they were friends.

'I told him George should have been a priority case. He's fitted him in on December the second, the day he goes back to the Central.'

Lauren was amazed. 'But should you? I mean, what if I'm wrong? What if he's just depressed?'

Eliot smiled at her. 'I trust your judgement—or rather your gut instinct. It's what a GP goes by and it's too valuable a gift to ignore.'

She took in a breath. She was so shocked that she could hardly speak. 'Well. . .thank you. I'm. . .flattered.'

He tugged open the door. 'Don't be. I knew four years ago what you were cut out for. I suppose I'm just giving myself a pat on the back for being right.'

If. . .if he had stayed a moment longer, she might well have thrown something at him, despite the lack of throwing material on her desk. Records were precious enough, despite the computer. And the computer was too heavy anyway.

The arrogant swine. He'd got George Viner in with Morris Leyton just to prove himself right—a four-year delay in proof too! Well, what made him think he was so right? she asked herself irritably as she prepared to leave on her calls.

She had wanted surgery with all her heart. She had focused on it for five years and then Eliot Powers had come along and she had almost let her career fly out of the window. The fact that she had been so desperately in love with him had obviously blinded her to reason and when he'd told her she'd be useless as a surgeon and then dropped her it had seemed like the end of her world. How could he live with that—and still tell her four years later that he had been right?

It was no thanks to him that she had put her life back together in Africa. As she went from visit to visit, she told herself that the certainty she had now that she was right for general practice had come through her own experience. She did interact well with people. She did have a gut instinct which she relied on.

She did care—care deeply. And she wanted to help— not just physically; she found enormous satisfaction in liaising, as she was now, with the district nurse in the case of an eighty-six-year-old arthritic lady, just discharged from hospital, who needed domiciliary care.

Providing that care with the help of social services and the nursing team, seeing the panic and desperation fade from her patient's eyes to be replaced with trust and appreciation, was something quite indefinable.

This wasn't achieved in surgery—or in vaccination programmes, where people briefly flitted in and out of medical vision. Here, in general practice, a bond was forged and if you were lucky, it was a strong and lasting link. General practice had changed indeed. OK, it wasn't the old traditional family health service of her parents' day, but the on-going challenge could be met with different techniques and, hopefully, better ones.

Her eighty-six-year-old would not be committed to a nursing home as she might automatically have been ten

years ago. Now there were services to back up home
care. And she, Lauren Kent, could help to make it
possible.

'She'd have just faded away,' the district nurse said
as they left the cottage. 'She was terrified we wouldn't
let her try to cope on her own after hospital.'

'Let's hope all goes well,' Lauren sighed as she
glanced back at the cottage. 'I'll call tomorrow and check
anyway.'

On the way home, Lauren tried one last time to put
her feelings into perspective. OK, so the truth was that
she had never been surgeon material and her career in
general practice was working out better than she could
have ever expected, but had Eliot had the right to tell
her in the way that he had four years ago?

One part of her said yes, he had—the part which was
not affected by the rejection he had made of her as a
woman. But the other half still hurt deeply at the manner
in which he had rejected her.

That she could have made such a mistake as denying
her real role merely because she hadn't wanted to follow
in her parents' footsteps seemed immature and childish.
But had she been just that when she'd been twenty-two?

She sighed. This soul-searching was a little too much
at the close of a busy day. Besides, admitting to that
meant she would have to admit to being wrong about
the man whose roof she now lived under, and she was
damned if she was going to give him that satisfaction.

In fact, she had very little time to think about anything,
since all logical brainpower shut down when she drove
up to Gorsehall Cottage and discovered a shiny, newly
registered red car parked outside. And just climbing out
of it was Caroline Peters.

CHAPTER SIX

'HI, LAUREN!'

'Hello, Caroline.' Lauren groped for her keys. 'Are you. . .going in?'

'Briefly.' She tugged a briefcase from the back seat and slammed her door. 'Business—unfortunately.'

Lauren slipped her key in the lock and pushed the door. She hadn't noticed Eliot's Rover, but then he could have put it in the garage.

Caroline sailed breezily into the front room and collapsed on the sofa. 'Oh, the fire's going in here,' she called. 'Eliot must be home.'

'Yes, I suppose he must.'

The phone rang then and Lauren hurried to answer it. She was on call until tomorrow lunchtime and this was a woman named Hilary Freen whose contractions had started.

'How far apart are they?' she asked after the woman had given her address, noticing as she scribbled it on the pad a long pair of jeans covered legs coming down the stairs. Eliot acknowledged her with a brief lift of his eyebrows and then disappeared.

Hilary Freen sounded breathless for a moment and then whispered, 'Oh God, my waters have broken.' And to Lauren's dismay the phone went dead.

She bent down and grabbed her case, only to be stopped by Eliot at the front door. 'What's up?' he asked as she hurried past him.

'Hilary Freen. Her waters have broken.'

'She's my patient. I'll take it.'

'I'm the duty doctor,' she responded waspishly as she

charged to the car. 'You have a guest, remember.'

'That's not the point, Lauren—'

Lauren didn't wait to hear what he had to say. The woman had sounded very distressed and then the phone had gone dead. Should she have phoned for an ambulance? Presumably Hilary Freen had someone with her. But what if she didn't? Still, the house was only two roads away; she could be there in less than a few minutes, swifter than an ambulance.

As she pulled up at the bungalow, it vaguely crossed her mind that Eliot had seemed concerned about this patient. Should she have agreed to his going? Had she just been upset by Caroline and reacted to his suggestion so snappily because of Caroline?

'Stop it, damn it!' she cursed under her breath, fed up with the continual self-analysis she seemed to be performing these days, most of it revolving around Eliot. She was the duty doctor. Emergency calls were her responsibility. That's all she had to think about now—a summing-up which proved accurate as she hurried up the bungalow path and found the front door open. She peered in and called.

'In here,' came a weak reply.

Lauren hurried in the direction of the voice, which she anticipated correctly as coming from the bedroom, and found Hilary Freen lying in a tangle of sheets and pillows on the double bed. She was trying to breathe and her hair was a damp mess as she lay back, sweat dripping from her forehead. 'I. . .I want to push!' she groaned.

Lauren slid her case and bag on the bedside chest of drawers, whipping out a maternity pack. 'Are you alone here?'

'Y. . .yes. My husband's on his way home.'

Lauren didn't stop to enquire further as she examined Hilary Freen and realised by the cervix that the birth was very close. Placing sterile sheets under the woman and donning her maternity gown, she ran to wash her hands, blessing the fact it was a bungalow with no stairs to contend with.

With a further examination of her patient, she found there wasn't a moment to lose. 'The baby's crowning, Mrs Freen. Now I want you to push when I say push and try to relax in between, remembering to do your breathing.'

The woman nodded and as each contraction came Lauren directed her to push and then encouraged her to conserve her energy until the next contraction, so combining the two forces to expel the baby safely without tearing the fragile tissue of the vagina.

'That's it, wonderful!' A tiny head emerged into the world, little eyelids knitted together. 'One more push, gently. . .yes!'

The cry was intoxicating. A beautiful, lusty, wonderful cry which filled the room and caused Hilary Freen to gasp in shock. 'Oh. . .darling baby!' She sank back as Lauren laid the child in her arms, and tears rolled down her cheeks. 'She's beautiful. . .so beautiful. . . Oh, God, I'm so lucky.'

Just then there was a noise from the hall and both women looked up. A tall, white-faced man stood there, a look of absolute astonishment on his face. 'Hilary?'

'It's all right Alan, Dr Kent delivered her safely. Oh, sweetheart, she's an angel!'

The husband rushed forward and sank onto the bed, his eyes devouring the scene with incredulity. Then both of them were in tears and Lauren found it difficult to restrain her own.

Alan Freen passed a hand across his eyes. 'It's a miracle. Oh, Lord, I just can't believe it!'

Hilary nodded wordlessly, cradling her little daughter in her arms.

Just then there was yet another movement at the door and Eliot appeared. Lauren frowned as he came in, shrugged off his outdoor coat and hurried over. 'I'm a little late, I see.' He grinned, arching black eyebrows. 'And who have we here?'

Both the Freens said, 'Angela,' and Eliot bent over, wreathed in smiles.

Was he checking up on her? Lauren wondered, suddenly angry. She gave him daggers as he glanced at her but he merely turned back to the baby and chuckled.

'I think we'd better just attend to the rest,' she said softly, turning her attention to Hilary. Alan Freen kissed his wife and daughter and then stood by Eliot. Out of the corner of her eye, she saw them shake hands before they moved into the hall, the sound of their voices tailing off as the door swung to.

With the cord clipped and cut thoroughly and the placenta delivered, Hilary Freen stayed Lauren's hand for a second. 'That was a close thing, wasn't it?'

Lauren smiled ruefully. 'But a perfectly normal delivery. May I have a look at her?'

'She's. . .she's all right, isn't she?'

Hilary Freen watched tensely as Lauren searched for abnormalities and discovered none. 'A perfect heartbeat, well-formed limbs and feet and healthy little hips, bright, shining eyes and a cloud of tufty white hair.' Lauren grinned. 'She's really beautiful.'

At that moment Eliot returned, dressed in a maternity apron, carrying a nursery bath of warm water. 'May I do the honours?'

Hilary giggled. 'I promised, didn't I?'

Without glancing at Lauren he took the child and washed her, so tenderly and lovingly that Lauren forced a lump down in her throat. She saw Hilary do the same thing and it was then she realised there was something quite special about this baby.

As if the surprise had registered on her face, Hilary explained. 'This is our second baby. We had a stillborn son sixteen months ago. I'm thirty-seven and Alan's forty. When he was conceived, we couldn't believe how lucky we were. But unfortunately. . .well, it's over now—but we shouldn't have tried again if wasn't for Dr Powers. He encouraged us all the way.'

Lauren swallowed, thankful that Eliot was absorbed with the baby and chatting to Alan and could not see her embarrassment. She understood his concern now over Hilary Freen and felt terrible that she had insisted on coming, but why hadn't he made more of an effort to stop her? 'I'm sorry it was me who came, Mrs Freen,' she apologised sincerely. 'I was unaware Dr Powers had a particular interest in your case.'

'Oh, please, it's just bliss that she has arrived, well and safely. I was dreading it. So was Alan. But it's all over now and I have you to thank for making it so easy for me.'

Lauren wished she could feel justified in her patient's thanks, but instead she felt as though she had encroached, even more so when, as soon as the detritus was cleared and little Angela lay in her mother's arms, washed and dried by Eliot, dressed in her first tiny gown by her father, she looked up to see Eliot's absorbed expression as the child began to suckle. Her greedy lips soon found the proffered nipple with a little help from Mum, who instinctively pushed her tiny head against her breast.

After endless cups of tea made by a highly excited new dad and the eventual arrival of the midwife, Lauren glanced at Eliot. He was heaving on his coat and she did likewise, beginning to feel the light-headed sensation of tiredness swim around in her head. They bade good-bye to the couple and a contented Angela snug in her warm white shawl.

'See you back at the house,' Eliot muttered as they walked to the cars, and Lauren hesitated, wondering if it was the appropriate time to offer the apology she knew she must. But he was already bending to climb into the Rover and she gave a defeated sigh and unlocked her own car.

Gorsehall welcomed them warmly, the embers of the fire still glowing in the grate. She slid off her things and slumped into a chair, waiting for him to come and join her, but instead, a few moments later, she heard him locking the front door. Then he shouted goodnight and she jumped to her feet, realising he had no intention of discussing the Freens with her.

'Are you going up?' she asked as she walked into the hall.

He nodded, his face drawn.

'Eliot. . .I want to apologise. I shouldn't have delivered Hilary Freen. I'm sorry.'

'Are you?'

'Of course I am. But I didn't know. You should have said.'

He eyed her with surprise. 'I tried, remember? But all I got was some sarcastic remark about Caroline. And quite frankly I didn't fancy a free-for-all standing there at the front door.'

She tried to hide her blush of shame. The arrival of Caroline had upset her and there was no getting away from it. 'I didn't mean to sound so snappy. . .'

'Then what did you mean? Heavens above, woman, Caroline was only calling on business.'

'I don't care why she was calling—'

'Yes, you do, or why else the puerile behaviour?'

That stung, and possibly because it had a ring of truth she glared at him defensively. 'I don't want a quarrel over this either, especially as I'm trying to apologise, but, since you mention it, I couldn't care less what you do with Caroline Peters—or, for that matter, whether she turns up on the doorstep every day of the week!'

'Really?' He paused, a contemptuous leer on his face. 'Strikes me you have one hell of an attitude problem for someone who says she doesn't care!'

'I don't have an attitude problem!' she almost shouted at him, realising she sounded like a fishwife, tried unsuccessfully to moderate her tone as it became an unreasonable whine. 'I was the duty doctor. I was on call. For all I knew, Hilary Freen wasn't a favoured patient.'

'I have no favoured patients,' he retorted calmly, 'and you'll find that out over the next few years, young woman, though you may well think you know it all at the moment. Favouritism doesn't come into it. All I was hoping for was a little luck, that I might have been able to follow the case along and be there at the birth. It wasn't a lot to ask, but it's not the end of the world it didn't happen. The baby arrived safely and that's all that matters.' He looked at her with resignation in his eyes. 'Now, I'm tired. You're tired. I suggest we try and get a little sleep.'

With mouth trembling, she watched him ascend the stairs. Why was he always so damnably logical? Why did he always make her feel like a child, berating her with a mixture of patience and disdain which made her feel about two feet high?

And worse, he had seen her reaction to Caroline. Had he guessed she had been jealous, had it shown? Why else tell her that Caroline had only visited on business?

Oh, God, I'm pathetic, she thought tiredly as she heard his door close upstairs and she dragged herself back to the fire and slumped once again in the chair. Her dark lashes fluttered closed as she drifted into slumber, even her humiliation unable to keep her awake.

At three o'clock in the morning, the phone rang and

someone asked for a visit. It was not the last by any means. By eight o'clock she had carried out two more—to a stroke and a post-op haemorrhage. By nine o'clock she hadn't slept a wink more and was back in surgery.

Of course, the trouble was, she had to eat humble pie over the following days, since she had to consult Eliot on practice procedure, or talk to him about cases, such as Polly Sharp's.

It was two days after the birth of Angela Freen, a beautiful, crisp, late November morning, when Polly Sharp walked into the surgery and collapsed. As she collapsed in Reception into Eliot's arms it was not surprising that he should help her, when she was recovered enough, into Lauren's consulting room.

He made her look almost doll-like as he helped her to a chair. Meanwhile, Lauren flicked through her records in search of what she hoped she would find—test results; she found none.

Polly, just surfacing and looking very white, smiled sheepishly. 'Sorry about that. I think I fainted, didn't I?'

Eliot grinned. 'You did it in the right place anyway. How do you feel?'

'Oh, a million dollars.' She laughed as she sipped water which Lauren had handed her. 'I feel a complete fool actually.'

'Have you eaten?' Lauren asked suspiciously.

The colour began to come back into her patient's face. 'Well. . .'

Eliot clucked his tongue. 'Naughty, naughty. Who's a bad girl?'

Polly responded, predictably, to his teasing. 'It's not much fun being good, Dr Powers; in fact it's crushingly boring!'

He frowned and gave a rueful grin, walking to the door.

'At least I went for those blessed tests a few days ago,' she sighed, looking to Lauren for support.

'Good!' Lauren decided she wasn't going to let her off that easily. 'At least that's a step in the right direction. But there's a way to go yet.'

Eliot hesitated, catching Lauren's gaze, and for a moment they stared at one another. Then he seemed to shrug back his shoulders and smiled at Polly. 'Well, I'll leave you to it, ladies.'

She gave him a flirtatious smile. 'Thank you for the rescue. I'll remember where to come and faint next time.'

He grinned and disappeared and Lauren sat down, wondering if he had the same effect on every female he met, remembering only too well the lascivious glances of the students at the training school and their envy when it had leaked out that she and Eliot were seeing one another.

'Wow!' Polly ejaculated, and Lauren jerked up her head, breaking from her reverie as she stared into Polly's curious gaze. 'Are you two an item by any chance?'

'No! Of course not!' Lauren bit down on her lip at her too-swift reply. 'Why do you ask?'

Polly giggled. 'Well, the air is pretty rarefied in here! And I am qualified to judge, having just fainted for lack of it!'

Lauren hedged. 'You should have eaten breakfast.'

'Stop changing the subject.'

'It was a long time ago, Polly. Really.'

'Not long enough,' Polly clucked. 'That guy is nuts about you.'

Lauren picked up the notes, avoiding eye contact. 'Rubbish! We're just colleagues—working on a very professional and temporary basis, I can assure you.'

The other woman sighed. 'And let me tell you, as a veteran of one failed marriage and two disastrous partnerships, I do happen to have learned one thing about men. They don't look like that guy looked when work is on their mind. He only had eyes for one person in this room and it wasn't me—unfortunately!'

Lauren flushed deeply. 'We aren't here to discuss me, Polly; it's you I'm concerned about. Come on now, let's see this list you have for me. Then perhaps we can see the true reason for your lack of rarefied air!'

They laughed, but Lauren was relieved when Polly finally produced a scribbled list of the foods she had eaten and those which seemed to have caused her digestive pain. It wasn't much to go on, but Lauren carefully directed her patient's mind towards IBS, rather than more personal matters which, it appeared, Polly preferred to discuss.

At last, they worked out a combination of foods and drinks which Polly promised to try to eat on a regular basis as a trial run. Lauren tried to explain yet again that time, travel, changes in routine and emotional stress could all influence the severity of her symptoms despite what she ate. Therefore all these areas of her life needed attention. But she had very little hope of Polly's paying much attention to her health if it were to challenge the structure of her high-flying career. The best she could hope for was that she would tolerate and sustain a regular diet in combination with the antispasmodic drugs.

When she had gone, Lauren paused over a coffee brought in by Jessie. Had the chemistry between her and Eliot been so obvious? Or maybe it was their antipathy which came across with resounding vibes? She knew that her own tension towards him was probably a defence barrier, but physical attraction was just what it intimated—an attraction of physical bodies—and, heaven help her, it was obviously still there and noticeable to other people—just as it had been four years ago when it had virtually wrecked her life.

Why couldn't she just turn it off? You could turn off
water, gas, electricity. Why not sexual appeal? It should
be easy. It should be. But every time he passed her,
looked at her, spoke to her something made the hairs on
her neck stand on end. Damn her miserable body! If
only it could be logical!

December broke with a week of rainbow skies, surprisingly warm, blustery weather and showers.

Charles Lee was getting into his stride and taking an
equal share of the night and weekend calls, but the viral
epidemic had translated into a flu outbreak and the visits
had been non-stop. Since delivering Angela Freen,
Lauren hadn't managed a complete night's rest. She was
on call one muggy evening, when, just as she was about
to leave, Chrissie Searle appeared in the waiting room
with an older man. Jessie asked Lauren if she would
see her.

Lauren slipped off her coat again and sat down, smiling at the couple who came in. But there was no smile
in return and the man, announcing himself as Chrissie's
father, stood aggressively beside a grey-faced daughter.

'How can I help?' Lauren asked pleasantly, sensing
trouble.

'You can't. You've already caused enough trouble.'
The man glowered.

'Dad!' exclaimed Chrissie on the verge of tears.

'And how is that, Mr Searle?' Lauren gestured to the
chairs but neither sat down.

'My girl isn't ready to have kids—and it's not up to
you to tell her she is! That's what the trouble is!'

'Mr Searle, Chrissie is old enough to judge for herself,
don't you think?'

'No, not if she's living under our roof, she's not.'

Lauren smiled at an obviously terrified Chrissie.

'I think your daughter has a voice of her own,' she said calmly.

The man strode forward and brought his fist down on the desk. 'Who exactly do you think you are to tell my daughter what to do?'

Lauren felt her tummy muscles tighten but she looked him directly in the eye. 'I've no intention of telling anyone what to do. Chrissie is an expectant mother and only she—and the father—can decide their baby's future.'

The man's face turned purple. 'You little—'

'I should calm yourself,' said a deep voice from the doorway, 'before you start saying things you will be sorry for, Mr Searle.'

They all looked up to see Eliot standing there. Chrissie burst into tears and the older man clenched his fists. 'Who the hell are you?' he demanded.

'I'm Dr Powers, Dr Kent's partner. Now, would you like to take a seat and talk this over sensibly or would you prefer to come back when you've calmed down?'

'I'll be blowed if I'll calm down. You're all the same,' Chrissie's father shouted. 'Do-gooders, the lot of you. Don't you know you're meddling? There isn't room for another kid in the house. What alternative have we got? He's not going to marry her—or look after the kid. It'll all come back on us!' He glared at both of them. 'Just keep your noses out of our affairs!' With that, he grabbed his daughter's wrist and pulled her out of the room.

'Poor Chrissie,' Lauren sighed as the door crashed.

'He does have a point, though.' Eliot dawdled over to the window, hands thrust deeply in pockets.

'About us being do-gooders?' she asked in surprise.

He leant against the wall and frowned. 'No. About it coming back on them. They're certainly a large family. Chrissie has two brothers and a younger sister. The house is pretty full.'

Lauren nodded thoughtfully. 'Yes, I see what you mean. Oh, dear. Do you know if Chrissie and David have worked anything out between them?'

He shook his head. 'Haven't seen him since.'

She stood and tiredly dragged on her coat. 'I wonder if I should call? Perhaps I could discuss the situation with the mother?'

'Bad news,' Eliot answered swiftly as he walked towards her to hand her her case. 'To interfere I mean.'

'But I'm not trying to interfere—'

'I know,' he cut in softly as she turned towards him. 'You mean well and you're worried for the girl, but you won't help matters by going there and getting embroiled in another argument. Wait for Chrissie to come to you.'

She paused and then looked up into the concerned blue eyes. 'No, I suppose you're right. I'd probably only exacerbate the situation.'

'It'll sort itself out—meanwhile, I've a favour to ask.' He smiled wryly, lifting his hands to pull out her collar and release her hair to fall over her shoulders. 'Don't look so suspicious,' he chuckled, and she couldn't help shivering at his touch as the pads of his fingers fleetingly brushed her neck. 'I heard from Professor Tomlinson's rest home this morning. He's very frail and last week he developed a chest infection. I'd like to go up there to visit him, perhaps stay the weekend. But it's a three-hour journey—somewhere near Oxford.'

'Oh, I'm sorry,' Lauren sighed and nodded. 'Yes, of course you must go. Have you told Hugo and Charles?'

'Not yet. I thought I'd mention it to you first.'

'I'm sure there won't be a problem. How old is the Professor now?'

'Eighty-one, but he's still articulate and mobile. Seeing him every month barely salves my conscience, though. It's at times like these I wish I was closer.'

She nodded, remembering the white-haired man

whom Eliot had introduced her to at St Margaret's,
when, even then, in his late seventies, he had managed
to continue with his famous lectures at training hospitals.

An orthopaedics specialist and a friend of Eliot's
father, he had taken over Eliot's education when his
parents had died in a tragic plane crash. Eliot had been
at boarding-school and he and his brother, Mark, who
now lived abroad, had continued with their education
under the auspices of Professor Tomlinson. Eliot and
the old man had remained close. Whether or not Eliot
had ever revealed their affair to him, she didn't know,
but he had always seemed sweet and kind to her, but
then, for all she knew, he had probably employed the
same courteous manner to all Eliot's women friends.

'When are you planning to go?' she asked, coming
back to the present as he opened the door for her.

'Tonight, if everyone's in agreement. That will give
me three whole days—if you feel you can cope here.'

'No problem.' She shrugged. 'Well, then, I probably
shan't see you. I've four or five calls to make.'

They stood staring at one another, his large body
seeming distant, his face shadowed as she lifted her
green eyes to his. For all she knew, he could be going
off for a long weekend with Caroline Peters. She
wouldn't put it past him. Though why he would want to
go about it that way she had no idea. However, she
didn't give a fig what he did with the woman or where
he went, so why dwell on it?

She was confident now in her general abilities as far
as the surgery went and she found herself beginning
to respond to general practice in a way which totally
surprised and elated her, giving her a sense of fulfilment
she had always hoped to find in a surgical career.

More than anything now, she wanted to make a
success of the practice. The problem was Eliot. It was
an irony that he had been proved right in so far as she

hadn't been right for surgery, but that made it no less difficult for her to accept him here, as partner in practice or as owner of Gorsehall.

And as she held onto this thought she found herself welcoming the three days' space in which to focus her mind and formulate her plans.

CHAPTER SEVEN

AT LEAST, that was the way she planned it.

As usual, the best-laid plans went askew and a Friday morning which was supposed to consist of Hugo and Charles and Lauren managing Eliot's surgery evenly between them turned out to be a morning of undiluted chaos.

Lauren arrived at the practice to discover Jessie, Robin and Jane furiously changing name-plates and reorganizing the appointment diary.

'Do you want the good or the bad news first?' Jane asked, ferrying an armful of records into Lauren's room.

'Surprise me,' Lauren grinned ruefully.

Jane sighed amiably. 'Right. The good news—we shall be seeing Dr Lee later in the day—hopefully. Though in what condition, I have no idea.'

'Charles?' Lauren realised she had only seen her and Hugo's names in Reception. 'What's happened?'

'Ah. The bad news. He's crushed his right hand in the up-and-over door on the garage. Apparently the index finger and thumb are broken. He's over in A and E and hyping on painkillers. But—' she shrugged '—he says he's coming in if it kills him.'

Lauren sank into her chair. 'It probably will.' She looked at the list for the morning—endless names. 'Look, Jane, tell him to stay at home after they've patched him up. He won't be any use to anyone in that condition. I'll stay in surgery until everyone's seen and cover his visits.'

'But what about tonight? It's Dr Lee's on-call weekend.'

94

Lauren shrugged. 'I'll cover. Perhaps the gods will give me a break.'

'But you did last weekend and you haven't really stopped—'

'Oh, it'll do me good. I need the practice.'

Jane narrowed her eyes. 'You certainly don't. You've done more than your fair share since you came home.'

Lauren smiled up at her. 'It was about time, wasn't it?'

Her practice manager looked embarrassed. 'Oh, God, what am I saying? I didn't mean to put my foot in it.'

'You didn't, Jane.' She grimaced. 'Mother could have done with my help a long time ago, I know. But there you are; all water under the bridge. Now I just want to put all my energies into doing the best I can here.'

'Well, that's good news. As a matter of fact it will be nice to be able to answer in the affirmative to our patients that the group will be going on as it is.'

Lauren frowned suddenly. 'I'm not sure it will, Jane. And I shouldn't like anything to be said yet. From my point of view, nothing is changing. But as far as Eliot and Hugo are concerned. . .' She gave a little shrug.

Jane looked crestfallen and then gave a deep sigh. 'I didn't know your mother, Lauren. Dr Grant and Dr Powers took me on after she died, but I do know she was a wonderful doctor—there are two and half thousand patients who say so. But I can honestly say that Dr Grant and Dr Powers have done wonders in her absence. It would be a sad day to see either of them leave.'

Lauren watched her slip out and close the door, surprised at the depth of feeling in Jane's remarks. As Jane had known Hugo for a long time Lauren could understand her attitude towards him, but Eliot was a relative newcomer. . . And it was obvious that she and Eliot couldn't both win the practice and they couldn't share it either. So what was the alternative?

With this thought, Lauren braced herself for the day.

Friday and Saturday passed in a whirl of activity; everyone ignored the glaring fact that they were short-staffed and asked for visits—some of them quite unnecessary as it turned out.

She put the rush down to pre-Christmas stress and was no nearer herself to defining her personal problems than she had been when Eliot had left on Thursday evening.

Charles was sporting a cast on his right hand, which luckily was not his writing hand. However, physical examinations would prove more of a hurdle and driving was out. That meant that with Eliot back on Monday, the three of them would have to cover Charles's visits.

Eliot phoned as Lauren dragged herself in the front door on Sunday lunchtime, her bones aching with exhaustion and her brain whirling from the call she had just made.

'You sound all-in,' he observed as she tried to smother a yawn.

'Oh, not really,' she mumbled. 'How is the Professor?'

A slight pause alerted her and Eliot's voice was husky as he answered. 'He passed away on Friday evening, quite peacefully.'

'Oh, Eliot,' she sighed. 'I'm sorry. Is there anything I can do?'

'No, not really. It's just that the funeral is on Wednesday morning...'

'And you'll want to stay there, of course.'

'It would help. He didn't have any close relatives and there's a great deal of sorting-out to be done. But I'll drive back tonight if there's a problem and go up again on Tuesday evening.'

She thought of the mind-blowing lists for Monday and Tuesday, of the forty-eight hours she had covered with only snatched sleep and Charles incapacitated and Hugo flat out—but in the end she decided to say nothing. After all, if she couldn't handle this, how would she cope with more exacting pressures? If she wanted general practice, this was it. Not a soft option by any means—and she certainly wasn't going to go whining to Eliot of all people.

'That's fine. Stay as long as you have to,' she said easily, and automatically stood to attention, pulling back her drooping shoulders as if he could see her. 'We'll cope.'

'You're sure?'

'Absolutely.'

She was proud of herself afterwards. She had shown him her mettle. All she had to do now was to survive the night and the next two days. Well, she could collect Charles and he could help with the surgeries. Anything he couldn't tackle he would have to send in to her or Hugo. The patients might not like it much, but they would understand once they knew the circumstances.

All she had to do was keep awake.

'Coffee,' she urged herself. 'Lots of it.'

Determinedly putting on the percolator and spoiling herself by turning on the central heating, she slumped into a chair, considering the tough brown roll and decidedly shabby-looking chunk of cheese she had discovered in the fridge.

She must shop.

And clean—a little. The place was covered in a veil of dust.

And there was washing-up in the kitchen.

The percolator grumbled and she poured herself a full mug. Setting it beside the cheese, she sat back in the chair and closed her eyes.

It was a fatal error. She awoke again three hours later to cold, oily-looking coffee and the insistent ring of the phone. Tom Clancey had chest pain.

Tom had suffered a particularly potent attack of angina and by the time she arrived he was fighting a headache too, an unfortunate side-effect of the Nitrolingual spray he had used.

Lauren examined him, listening to the recovering beat of his heart and watching the colour seep slowly back to his face. 'Tough one this time, was it, Tom?' she asked gently.

He nodded, slumped in an armchair. 'And now I've had to use that thing!' He glowered contemptuously at the spray on the table. 'I've got such a blasted headache, I can't think straight.'

Lauren smiled wryly. 'Don't you normally use it when you have an attack?'

He shrugged. 'Not if I can help it. I detest headaches almost as much as I do angina.'

'I'm afraid it's an unfortunate side-effect.' She curled the cloth around his arm and took his blood pressure. 'And your tablets? Last time I saw you, I gave you atenolol. How are you finding them?'

He glanced at her and shrugged again.

'You haven't persevered, have you?'

'Well. . .not much. . .I lost the prescription as a matter of fact.'

She took out her pad and wrote, handing it to him firmly. 'This time, do as I say. One tablet each day and there are twenty-eight tablets. I expect to see you in a month, when I'll make out another prescription and check you over. I've prescribed another Nitrolingual spray for you to carry in your truck. When you have the angina, spray the dose under your tongue—no delaying it, now. Then close your mouth immediately after the dose.'

He nodded reluctantly. 'You're worse than your mother was.'

She smiled ruefully. 'I'll take that as a compliment. And—if you have another severe attack I'm going to whip you in.'

He snorted. 'I only had my last check-up three months ago!'

She ignored this. 'You could also do with losing a little around the waistline—and cutting down on your hours. And don't tell me you're in semi-retirement, because I won't believe you. I've seen your truck around Gorsehall more often than I've seen the bus services!'

'That's not saying much,' he grunted in good humour. 'Diabolical, they are.'

'Well, let this be a warning, Tom. Stick to your medication, ease off the brew at the local and—'

He held up his hands, grinning. 'OK, point taken. Thanks for coming, Lauren. Bit much on a Sunday, calling you out.'

She smiled at him warmly. 'Any time, Tom. But the less I see you professionally the better. Socially, of course, it's a pleasure.'

'Do you know, your mother would be proud of you.' He stood up, slowly, studying her. 'She was never one to beat about the bush either.'

She knew he meant kindly. 'You must have known her well, Tom.'

'Aye, that I did. We were good buddies.'

She hesitated at the front door of the old woodman's cottage set behind the village garage and wondered if her mother had often come here to share private chats, as well she could imagine them doing. 'As a point of interest, what do you think of the practice now?' she asked curiously.

'Brilliant,' he responded quickly. 'Your mother never resisted change. She was very forward-thinking. But she waited a long time to bring someone in from the outside. She said she always had you to thank for that.'

'Me?'

He nodded. 'You introduced her to Dr Powers.'

'Oh. . .I see.'

'We were all a bit dubious at first, I have to say. Smart new quack, we thought. All talk and no action. Or the reverse—all go and no bedside manner—equally bad for the village. But he turned out a good 'un. In more respects than one.'

Lauren refrained from commenting. Why was it that at every turn she seemed to discover something about Eliot that forced her to revise her opinion? But, no matter what anyone said, the way that Eliot had shut her out of his life four years ago, so callously, so hard-heartedly, was inexcusable. She had to remember this, for above all else she was determined not to be hurt again.

With the firmest of intentions, she arrived back at Gorsehall Cottage. The watery sun was bouncing against the lattice windows, the eaves as usual full with brittle, papery leaves, and as she walked into the house it seemed a little lost.

Almost instantly the phone rang. Someone had a bout of flu in the Dip and was so agitated that all her reasoning over the phone failed to resolve his anxiety. She traipsed off again, closing her mind to the perspiration that had started at the nape of her neck. But by the time she returned from seeing her flu victim safely tucked up in bed with a hot-water bottle she herself was sweating profusely.

Sleep overcame her until midnight, when another call came and she hauled herself into the night, shivering like a jelly. By Monday she thought she felt a little better, having had five hours' solid sleep. But during the congested morning she felt queasy and clammy again.

Luckily Hugo was on call that evening and at teatime she left early and just about managed to get home before she collapsed. During the night, she had terrible dreams and woke in a pool of sweat. Somehow she dragged herself into work on Tuesday morning, but her surgery was a nightmare and by lunchtime she felt decidedly ill.

'You look gruesome,' Hugo told her, and waved her out of her room.

He packed her off without argument and Charles threatened her with his good hand, reminding her she was not indispensable.

In bed she trembled violently and felt horribly nauseous. Though her sensible, logical mind tried to reject it, the dread which had been growing for the last few hours now materialised into a tangible fear.

Was this a bout of malaria?

It couldn't be! Her tests had shown that she had been attacked by Plasmodium falciparum in Africa, one of the four species of Plasmodia that affect human beings. It had been a crucifying attack and very serious, landing her in the Tropical Disease Centre. But after treatment she had been told there would be no recurrence. . .could they have been wrong?

Lauren remembered hardly anything after this. Her mind lapsed into a kind of limbo, shutting out the outside world. She was barely conscious of where she lay. Her body ached in every muscle. She couldn't get warm enough one minute and then she was too hot the next.

In the darkness, she fumbled for the light and then it was too glaring and in her clumsy effort to turn it off she knocked it over and it shattered on the floor, china and glass bulb everywhere.

With no strength left she gave up trying to get out of bed to clear it. She would leave it until the morning. But her temperature soared and she sank into a strange,

102   PERFECT PARTNERS

murky world of shivering semi-consciousness as her
body finally capitulated to the fever.

Lauren licked her dry lips which tasted salty. With
aching determination she forced open her lids. The sun
was shining into the room, the bed was made with fresh
covers, cool and untangled, and she lay in the middle of
it, her head propped on a smooth wall of pillows. Her
eyes automatically flashed down to the floor. The
light—the last thing she clearly remembered—had disappeared.

Managing to move her stiff neck, she groaned.

'Ah, you're awake!'

She started and saw Eliot standing at the door.
'You're. . .you're home?'

He walked to the bed, dressed in casual green cords
and a green sweatshirt. He sat on the bed beside her, his
bulk so heavy that both she and the mattress dipped in
a curve. He held a bowl of soup in one hand and a spoon
in the other. 'Chicken broth—my speciality. Egg custard
for afters.'

Lauren remembered vaguely someone else telling her
about chicken soup and egg custard and it having some
connection with Eliot.

'You know, I'm beginning to enjoy unravelling you
from precarious situations,' he told her as she struggled
to sit up. 'Except that this latest one was a touch too close
for comfort. Do you know, you almost started a fire?'

'Oh, heavens!' She closed her eyes again. 'The bedside light.' When she flicked them open he was
frowning at her.

'Lucky the thing fused, but not before singeing the
carpet.'

'Oh, Lor'.' She looked down and, true enough, there
was a burn mark right in the middle of the carpet.

He sighed. 'Why not tell me I was needed here,

Lauren? What on earth possessed you to keep me in the dark? I could be very cross with you—if you hadn't been so ill.'

She looked, she hoped, unrepentant. 'We were coping, but—'

'But Charles smashed his hand up, there was another outbreak of flu in the village, you couldn't have got one good night's rest—and then you collapsed. Yes, I would say you did very well in my absence.'

'We did—at first!'

'Do you know it's Friday?'

'F-Friday?' She sat up and cringed as her head felt as though it had come off and had been stuck back on with superglue.

He curved his hands around her shoulders. 'Lie back.'

'But—'

'But nothing! Hugo and I arranged With Dr Lowry from the next village to help us out for a week. We'll return the favour when you are well. We've had to do it before and no doubt we shall do it again.'

She sank back, sighing deeply. 'How long have you been here?'

'I found you on Wednesday afternoon. You were delirious as a fool.'

She bit her lip, a shadowy recollection coming over her.

'You've had a monster bout of flu—possibly because you ignored the symptoms in the first place. You must have felt ill over the weekend and kept it to yourself, you crazy woman.'

She was too weak to argue.

'I didn't realise my presence was having such an adverse effect on your life; that you were so keen to be rid of me you became one of the walking dead.'

She said nothing, obediently sipping the broth he fed her.

'Well, you're on the mend now. In a few days you should be right as rain—though more by luck than judgement, I have to say.' He stood up, the tray in his large hands, and he walked to the door.

'Eliot?'

He glanced back, brows raised.

'Thank you,' she managed reluctantly. He gave her an amused grin and closed the door. She sank back, feeling fractionally better. Even in her delirium, all her miseries had abounded: the malaria, the news of her mother's death, the awful void when she'd come back home and the problems that had followed. But the lethargy was leaving her and she closed her eyes and slept peacefully, for the first time in weeks.

'Why the hell didn't you tell me about the malaria?' He was so furious that she turned away from him.

'Because. . .because—oh, I don't know. I suppose I thought it sounded so pathetic. You hear all sorts of excuses—'

'For not attending funerals?'

'For not accepting responsibility.'

He shook his head. 'The way you clammed up was bound to make me think that! Damn it, Lauren, if you hated the sight of me at least you owed Hugo an explanation.'

'I know. And I'm sorry.'

'Wise after the event,' he sighed.

She stared down at her hands. They were sitting in front of the fire and she had had no option but to tell him about the malaria. If it had just been the flu, she could go back to work, but she must be sure it was that—just flu.

'You're only confessing now,' he growled at her, 'because I've taken a blood test, aren't you?'

She nodded out of shame. 'But you could have asked me first—'

'About the blood test?' he demanded. 'No way. You'd have put up an argument and frankly I was worried you were anaemic; you're far too thin and you don't eat. I had my doubts as to whether you were. . .'

She lifted a wry brow. 'Anorexic?'

'I did consider it a possibility.'

'Which is why you sneaked a blood test whilst I was out of it?'

He shrugged. 'As your doctor I considered it necessary.'

She couldn't argue with that and decided she would give in as gracefully as she could whilst she was winning. 'Well, I'm telling you the whole truth now. And I'm not anorexic. I just lost loads of weight with the malaria and it's never gone back on again, no matter how much I seem to eat.'

He regarded her with a deep frown and stroked his chin with thoughtful fingers. 'Plasmodium falciparum you say? All the organisms are released into the liver and the bloodstream at the same time, aren't they?' His face darkened at her slow nod. 'Well, you must have had a pretty rotten time—but at least you should have only one bout with that type.'

'Hopefully yes. Though I was beginning to wonder.' She tilted her head. 'And the Professor's funeral?'

He shrugged. 'Poorly attended for such a great old character. He had no family and I think he'd outlived most of his peers.'

She sighed. 'But at least you were with him and that's a comfort.' She would have given anything to have been with her mother during the closing moments of her life, better still, the last months, and she still felt deeply distressed that she hadn't been there.

She gazed up into the eyes which were studying her

carefully and she suddenly shivered at the warmth that was reflected in them, and then in one economical movement he had come across and slid his arm around her and pulled her down onto the firm, hard rise and fall of his chest.

CHAPTER EIGHT

'YOU were an idiot, you know, not telling me,' Eliot scolded mildly. 'I wonder if you realise just how ill you've been? You know, it could have turned to pneumonia. If I hadn't come back no one would have been any the wiser.'

Lauren found herself melting into the warmth of his body, unable to resist the invitation of his fingers kneading softly through her hair as he cradled her against him.

'I'm sorry,' she mumbled. 'I thought I could cope. I didn't want to let anyone down.'

He sighed, lifted her legs up from the draught on the floor and laid them across his lap. 'I think you'd better make the most of your recuperation and nip back into bed for a few hours,' he said, and she nodded, but they remained there and suddenly she knew she didn't want to go anywhere—not anywhere; she just wanted to stay here in his arms like this.

'Don't look at me like that, with those huge, innocent eyes of yours,' he muttered as she realised she had been devouring him with her gaze. 'Not if you want to stay safely wrapped up in that blanket.'

But she didn't want that, did she? she admitted to herself swallowing. And she felt the air between them tense and her heart began to beat so rapidly that she had to suck in her breath and swallow again, only very hard, in order to breathe.

'Lauren. . .' His voice was low and husky.

She was afraid he would move, but instead he looked down at her, smoothing her hair away from her face, so

107

that her green eyes stared up at him and her lips opened
involuntarily.

She watched him numbly, too aroused to speak, and
she saw the same depth of desire glittering in his eyes, the
same need and want that was coursing through her body.

'Oh, damn this,' he swore softly, and as though he
was fighting against every instinct he cupped her face
in his hands with fingers that trembled against her skin
and brought down his lips to cover the smooth, creamy
invitation of her mouth. And to her astonishment her
hands came out of the blanket she had wrapped around
her and slid to his neck and up into his hair and, pulling
him down, she gave way to the longing that she had pent
up for so long.

She shifted against him, levering herself into his
warmth, and his hands came to help her, sliding below
the blanket, and as his kiss grew deeper his fingers
slowly picked open the slit of her nightdress and
smoothed in to the warm skin that lay beneath.

Lifting his face, he stared at her, beginning to caress
the swell of her breasts and the delicate, hardening
nipples which responded with immediacy to his touch
like tiny, flowering buds kissed by the sun.

'You are so beautiful, Lauren, so hard to resist,' he
murmured, and he pulled her against him, so that she
felt the hard thrust of his arousal and knew that she was
flying along the road which said no return. Don't be hurt
again, a voice whispered; don't let it happen. . .

But I want it to happen, she answered, honestly for
once. I want him and I need him and all these years I've
been lying to myself, playing a part.

A low groan came from the base of his chest as his
head came down to snuggle into her neck, kissing her
with soft butterfly kisses down to the opened flap of her
nightdress, and he took the small pink buds in his mouth,
caressing them until he brought them to fragile, aching

peaks which demanded her surrender as her mouth opened to a burning, shuddering gasp of need.

'Lauren, for God's sake, stop me. . .' he groaned raggedly as somehow he was lying with her on the settee, their bodies melding with heat. 'I gave you my word. . .'

Her eyes went up to him and she saw the same longing that she knew was reflected in hers and she had no power to stop him, nor did she want him to stop.

'You've been ill. . .you're vulnerable. It's my fault. . .' He moaned, suddenly holding her wrists and preventing her from touching him.

'It's no one's fault,' she whispered, and her heart sank as he suddenly stiffened beside her and released her wrists and drew together the delicate edges of her nightgown.

'I shouldn't have let this happen.' He hung his head and scraped back his black hair with his hands and she felt the brief tremble of his body. 'Sit up, my sweet,' he murmured softly, and she let him help her as he tucked the blanket around her and avoided her eyes, and she clenched her hands as though for the last ten minutes she hadn't known what she was doing. 'Just let me hold you for a moment and then I'm going to take you back to bed—to sleep and to get well.'

He turned her against him, settling her once more into the crook of his arm, and, drawing the tendrils of her dark hair behind her ears, he kissed her gently on her forehead.

Tomorrow would she think she was crazy to have let this happen, when tonight it had seemed so right? If he had wanted to make love to her she would have let him. It was he who had stopped, not she.

And by the way her body was burning and her heart was pounding she could not say she had stopped wanting him, and she would be an even greater fool to imagine that tomorrow she would feel any different.

It was some days later, when she was making her way back to Gorsehall Cottage from a busy afternoon at surgery, that she realised how much she was beginning to look forward to Eliot's company. The sudden realisation came as a shock and she wondered if her feeling this way had anything to do with what had happened between them since her illness.

The night that he had sat with her in front of the fire, she had been so willing, her body had craved him and he must have known it and yet. . .yet he had held back. He had not made love to her; instead, he'd packed her off to bed and brought her a warm drink and left her to sleep in peace. Even now her cheeks flushed when she thought of how ready she had been to make love. And yet, he hadn't let it happen. . .

Sighing, becoming frustrated by her thoughts, she drove in to the cottage parked in the garage and told herself she would occupy the evening with as many jobs as she could. Eliot was on call and had marked several visits in the appointments diary, so she knew she had the place to herself and wouldn't be disturbed much before ten.

The after-effects of the flu had left her a little shaky but on the whole she was feeling good and the idea of making a Christmas shopping list appealed. Just as she had let herself in, having resolved to do just that, the phone rang.

'Lauren,' said Hugo hesitantly when she answered it, 'I'm sorry to bother you but it's rather important. Have you an hour spare? It's nothing I can discuss over the phone. Do you think you could meet me somewhere for a drink?'

In just under an hour, Lauren was waiting in the Moon and Sixpence, warmed by the pub's open fire, and Hugo arrived, rather out of breath. 'Sorry about this, Lauren. Drink?'

She gestured to her glass. 'I've a fruit juice, Hugo, but order yourself something.'

He returned a moment later with a half-pint. 'Now,' he sighed, sinking into a seat next to her and taking a gulp, 'I think I'd better get straight down to business.' He paused and patted his top lip with a rumpled handkerchief. 'You know that I've been considering retirement... And with Christmas coming up Amy would like to know if we can celebrate this as the last year of on-call, if you see what I mean?'

Lauren sighed and nodded, well aware of what he was trying to tell her in his clumsy fashion. 'Hugo, I shall miss you dearly, but I understand you need time with your family, who have had to put up with seeing so little of you over the years. As for my part, I can only reassure you I've never been more certain of what I wanted to do, and that, of course, is to continue in practice.'

He sat back and sighed. 'That's a relief, then, Lauren. I didn't want to spring a bombshell on you as I wasn't sure about you...and...er—'

'Eliot.' Her voice was unsteady as she said his name.

He nodded. 'My dear, I understand you and Eliot have had problems in the past. Eliot explained before he took on the partnership. He said that although he was very fond of you you had decided to go your separate ways and, with that in mind, he was deeply concerned over your reaction to his involvement in the surgery.'

'Well,' she sighed, resting back in her chair, 'that's one way of putting it, I suppose. To be honest, I didn't think when I came back from Africa there was any future for us in the same practice. However, Eliot persuaded me into a six-month trial partnership...' She gave a small shrug, unable to quantify her thoughts to Hugo.

However, he nodded and rubbed his chin thoughtfully.

'Which is why I asked to see you in private. I think it's only fair to offer you my share of the partnership in view of the long years your mother and I spent building it up after your father's death, even though Eliot has put his heart and soul into it since becoming the third partner.'

Lauren realised that Hugo must have been worried about this and she warmed to him for his loyalty. She should have been relieved that the opportunity was being presented to her; after all, if she took it she would then be in a powerful position, owning two thirds of the practice, but instead, with some surprise, she heard herself refusing.

'I appreciate your offer, Hugo, but I don't want to go behind Eliot's back in any way. He did hurt me once, a long time ago, and if I were holding a grudge I think I'd take you up on your offer. But I feel the best way to handle your retirement is to bring it up at the next practice meeting, don't you?'

There was obvious relief on Hugo's face and she knew it must have been a great ordeal for him to say what he had. Spurred by affection for him, she leant across and kissed him on the cheek. 'Enjoy your Christmas, Hugo, and tell Amy she can confidently celebrate your last working Christmas.'

He gave a great guffaw and went decidedly pink. 'I think this calls for another drink,' he declared, and they both laughed as he got up to go to the bar.

Lauren watched him go and did not know whether to be pleased with herself for acting so nobly or to kick herself for being a fool.

On the way home, Lauren decided she would forget the shopping list, make herself a meal and wallow in a bath. But when the phone rang at nine-thirty she had barely begun to eat, having attended to half a dozen odd jobs first.

'I've had a call from the Professor's solicitor in Oxford. There are a few loose ends to tie up,' Eliot told her, 'and as it's the weekend I thought I might drive up tonight. Charles will take calls. Do you need me for anything?'

'No, I don't think so,' she answered thoughtfully, wondering where he was phoning from. 'What about a change of clothes and a meal?'

There was another pause as he cleared his throat. 'I've eaten and I've an overnight bag in the car which I collected earlier; you weren't in.'

She suddenly experienced a guilty pang as she thought of her impromptu rendezvous with Hugo and for no good reason she found herself answering evasively. To compound this, the line seemed to have gone dead and she realised she had brushed her elbow on the phone and disconnected them. On the point of re-dialling, she realised she didn't know where he was.

First, she tried the surgery, and then when she received no reply she put her hand to her head. He would, of course, be at Caroline's. But she didn't know Caroline's number, and even if she had she would not have phoned him there.

Having eaten only a small snack after all, she bathed and sat on the edge of her bed, staring at the phone. He hadn't rung back. She drank her milk, decided she was too tired to read and switched off the light.

Sleep evaded her. The wakeful part of her brain listened for all the usual sounds which weren't forthcoming: the plumbing and the water flushing, sounds of whistling in the kitchen, logs being chopped for the fire—an infuriating habit he had very often late at night. Once or twice she had peeked out and seen him thrashing away in the light of the garage, stacking the logs in piles along the solid walls.

She found, annoyingly, that the silence grated on her.

Visions of Caroline and Eliot travelling up to Oxford together forced her to sit up and switch on the light. She tuned into her pocket radio, clamping the earphones on her head.

They were playing carols and finally, just before she took the earphones off, she heard 'White Christmas' and swallowed irritably on the lump in her throat.

'No good feeling sorry for yourself,' she mumbled into the pillow as she buried her head in it.

Because she didn't want to give in to watching the television over the cold and rainy Sunday, Lauren surveyed her list of Christmas cards. She dutifully unwrapped the two boxes she had bought in the village and wrote, stamped and addressed them. Her Christmas shopping she would squeeze into one day at the new gift shop which had opened in Gorsehall. The thought struck her that it might be open on a Sunday so close to Christmas and she threw on her coat and hauled out the Saab from the garage.

By three in the afternoon when she returned home she had virtually crossed every name off her present list. Books, cosmetics, linens and stationery filled the back seat of the car. Industriously, and ignoring the sudden tiredness which came over her, she ferried them from the garage to the warm front room.

Intending to wrap, label and put them away, at six she realised she had no energy left and piled everything in a corner for another day. Succumbing to temptation, she switched on the television and watched a Christmas show. It deflected her thoughts from Eliot for a good half-hour and then she switched it off and gazed from the window at the dark, rainy night.

Would he be home soon? she wondered. The house seemed unfamiliarly cold even though she had built a blazing fire. By ten, the television was on again, but she wasn't listening to a word. She was listening instead for the hum of an engine and waiting for the reflection of lights through the window.

But they never came.

'Morning!' Jane called as Lauren walked into her room on Monday. 'We've a massive pre-Christmas rush; list's on your desk.'

Lauren sank into her seat with a sigh, on her right, an array of memos, on her left, the computer winking at her wildly.

'Any special problems?' She sipped the cup of tea Jane had brought her.

'Where would you like me to start?' Jane laughed. 'And have you got all day?'

Both women giggled and Lauren sat back, curling her long dark hair up into a businesslike bunch at the back of her head, sticking in a few pins to secure it. 'OK, fire ahead. Have we a full complement this morning, by the way?'

'Thank the Lord, yes.' Jane placed a pile of records in front of her. 'Dr Lee is hoping to have his plaster removed some time this week and Dr Grant has the Christmas rota in his room, praying for a miracle.'

Lauren lifted her brows. 'Well, you can tell him he's got one. I'm volunteering for duty over the holiday.'

Jane's mouth fell open. 'Are you sure? I was going to try to stagger the rota.'

'Don't bother. I think I owe everyone a Christmas off this year.'

The practice manager sighed, lifting her shoulders heavily. 'Well, it makes my job a lot easier, but I don't like to think of you taking it on single-handed.'

Lauren dismissed it quickly and frowned. 'Dr Powers isn't here, is he, by the way?'

Jane nodded. 'He was in before me—and I arrived at

seven-thirty this morning to do a bit of catching up.'

'Was he? That's odd. He must have come straight down from Oxford.'

'Life is made up of little oddities,' Jane laughed softly. 'Not always ours to reason why, either.'

Lauren grinned. 'Too profound for me at this hour of the morning, I'm afraid. Now, what have we got here?'

'Test results.' Jane shuffled the letters. 'George Viner's and Polly Sharp's. I'll leave them with you.'

'Has anyone else looked at them?'

Jane nodded. 'Eliot—and he said you'd probably want to see them straight away.'

She smiled. 'OK, Jane, thanks. I've half an hour before my first patient, I see, so I'll plough through them as quickly as I can.'

'Ring up to me if you want correspondence written. I'll get it off promptly because of the Christmas post.'

In the silence of her room, Lauren studied the first report, from Morris Leyton, and sighed, leaning back in her chair. When she had thoroughly digested it, she read the second, Polly's.

Just then a shadow fell across her and she looked up. Eliot nodded and gave her a brief smile. Though he was dressed smartly as usual and wearing a formal grey suit and tie, his hair was slightly ruffled and his eyes looked tired. An energetic weekend with Caroline? she wondered.

'You've Polly Sharp there?' he said, coming to look over her shoulder.

'Yes, the results revealed no abnormalities, I'm pleased to say. You've seen them, Jane said.'

He nodded. 'Your IBS was pretty accurate,' he said briskly. She smelt his distinctive odour, a musky blend this morning, rather bland, not quite the same potency of aftershave that he usually used. Was it one he used for Caroline's delectation? she found herself speculating. 'And George Viner. . .?' he asked, frowning.

She lifted the report. 'It proves George has a biological problem, at least.'

He nodded, glancing over it. 'The scan of his brain reveals some damage—here—which Maurice concludes he must have incurred from the pole incident, though Lord knows how it happened. George himself doesn't seem to remember, does he?' He bent down, tracing a finger over the scan results, briefly touching her hair with the lapel of his suit. 'It shows the blood flow within the brain. . .here. . .and here. There's a pattern of abnormality on the left side, where we saw the contusion, just over the temporal occipital region and possibly the cerebellum.'

She swallowed hard to offset the shiver down her spine as his body touched her again. 'The structure at the b-base of the brain involving movement,' she confirmed stumblingly. 'Hence George's problems with his riding abilities. No wonder he thought he was. . .er. . . going mad.'

'The motor skills are obviously impaired,' he agreed, rubbing the faint shadow of stubble on his chin. 'Plus the gaps in his memory. . . At least now he'll have a tangible reason for his memory loss and disrupted coordination. The chances for complete recovery are fair, I'd say. It might take many weeks, though—and encouragement from his family will be an important part of the recovery process.'

She moved from him, forcing a calmer note into her voice. 'How about physiotherapy?'

He nodded. 'Absolutely.'

She looked up at him and their eyes locked and for one moment she couldn't think of a reasonable thing to utter, knowing that what she wanted to say—that she had missed him more than she had ever thought possible—was very far removed from what she should be about to say professionally about George Viner.

How long they looked at one another, she didn't know; suddenly Jessie swept in and Lauren managed to clear her throat as she looked into Jessie's startled face.

'Oh, I'm sorry, Dr Kent; I didn't realise you were with Dr Powers.'

'It's all right, Jessie. How can I help?' Lauren took the opportunity to rise and move away from the tall body which had decided not to move very far, despite the sudden appearance of the receptionist.

Jessie looked flustered. 'Oh, your first two have arrived. Shall I hold them off for a while?'

Lauren glanced up at the tall figure beside her desk. 'No. . .er. . .is there anything else, Eliot?'

'Nothing important,' he said, and smiled and gestured with his dark eyes to Jessie to go ahead.

'Mrs Hewlitt, then,' she said, and quickly scampered from the room.

Mrs Hewlitt came dashing in and almost collided with Eliot.

He smiled, stepped back and allowed the woman through, arching a brow at Lauren on the way.

She tried not to look as flustered as she felt, hoping Mrs Hewlitt would not see the flush rising up in her cheeks, or the slight tremble in her fingers, which she hid well beneath the desk whilst she tried to concentrate on her patient's problems.

The run-up to Christmas was frantic.

Fortunately Charles was freed from his cast and Hugo was in excellent spirits after he was able to confirm a long and uninterrupted holiday with his family. Lauren found time to buy a tree and bring it into the cottage, but her plans to decorate it had to be shelved as a pre-Christmas influx of sore throats and coughs hit the surgery.

Hugo was so relaxed that it seemed to spill off onto everyone else and her inner confidence grew, making her surprisingly at ease with Eliot, who when he saw her, which was mostly early in the morning before they left for surgery, was looking more tired and strained than she had ever seen him.

Caroline? she wondered, and was convinced when she saw the girl turn up at the surgery and ensconce herself with him. Nor was she surprised on several occasions to discover that Eliot had not returned home overnight.

Lauren tried twice to contact George Viner. Eventually she called to see him, the week before Christmas. The stables looked empty, without a horse in sight. Shirley Viner walked across a deserted yard and took her into the house, which still had tarpaulin over the roof.

'I've tried to ring you,' Lauren said, noticing the bleakness of the kitchen.

Shirley sighed and sat down, throwing her coat over the chair and tugging off her boots. Finally, she looked up at Lauren, her eyes filled with tears. She put her head in her hands and cried freely. 'It's George,' she sobbed. 'He's left me.'

Lauren sank down onto a chair beside her. 'But why?'

'It just got too much for him, I suppose.' She pulled out a handkerchief and blew her nose. 'The bank is calling in our loan.'

'Is there no way you can avoid it?'

The distraught woman shook her head. 'No. The feed merchants have stopped dealing with us—the vet, the blacksmith, everyone to whom we owe money. I'm selling the stock and paying off what creditors I can. Then. . .' she shrugged. . .'it's anyone's guess.'

'Do you know where George is?'

She shook her head. 'He left a note. Said it was just too much, that we'd be better off without him.'

'Do the police know?'

'Yes. But there's nothing much they can do except circulate his description.'

Lauren sighed. 'I'm so sorry. I wish I'd managed to get you sooner. George's tests have come through and show the reason for his behaviour. He must have sustained an injury—it is biological and he isn't going insane.'

The shocked woman stared at Lauren whilst she told her the details. Then the two women sat in silence and Lauren tried to think of something she could do or say to help. But if George had disappeared then there was no way of helping him.

'And the children?' she asked eventually.

'Gone to my sister for Christmas. They'll be better off there with their cousins.' She pulled back her shoulders and stared abstractedly through the window. 'I don't know whether to hate or miss George. I think I was beginning to hate him, Dr Kent, for all the trouble he'd landed us in. But if there is a reason for it—well, I suppose he deserves sympathy.'

Lauren hesitated, wondering how the poor woman was going to cope. 'Mrs Viner, if your husband registers with another doctor we might be able to trace him.'

There was a brief look of hope and Shirley Viner bravely wiped her face and stood up. 'Yes, that's true. Still, in the meantime, life goes on, doesn't it?'

Much saddened by her visit to the Viners', Lauren drove back to the surgery. It was the last Friday before Christmas and the girls had put up the decorations and a small tree in the corner by the children's play area.

Lauren sighed as she gazed around her. It just didn't seem fair to have to struggle so desperately at this time of year, but then even Shirley Viner was fortunate in comparison with some of the people in the Third World—a thought which did nothing to enliven her as she saw Polly Sharp sitting in the waiting room.

Lauren smiled, disengaging herself from her unhappy ruminations, and beckoned her in. 'How are you?' she asked, dismayed to see her patient looking so ill.

Polly shrugged. 'To be honest—awful. I've been trying everything to get rid of the pain—acupuncture, reflexology, relaxation—but nothing's helped. Last week I almost gave up. I just couldn't drag myself into work and took time off.'

Lauren shed her coat and flicked on her monitor on the desk. 'The tests failed to reveal any abnormality,' she explained carefully, 'which means we can safely exclude the possibility of any infection or underlying disorder. But it still means we are left with the IBS. How are you faring with your diet?'

Polly grimaced. 'I avoid the things which seem to cause me discomfort, but I still can't do without the painkillers. When I tried to stop, the pain was uncontrollable. I'm beginning to get desperate, Dr Kent.'

Lauren glanced at her notes. 'There is an alternative. . .' She looked up thoughtfully. 'A clinic I could refer you to. I won't say it's a sure-fire cure because it isn't. And the treatment is fairly new—a psychologist teaches coping strategies and the physio improves fitness, amongst other things. Really it's a question of coming to terms with pain and coping with it.'

'Doesn't sound particularly impressive,' Polly sighed. 'Am I going to have this all my life? This last year has been a nightmare.'

Lauren hesitated. 'With an irritable colon the waves of muscular contraction are irregular and uncoordinated— this interferes with the faecal matter passing through the intestine. The cause of the disorder is not fully understood, unfortunately. Like indigestion, we think it's most likely a combination of factors.'

'Wonderful,' Polly sighed again. 'In other words, there's no cure.'

'There is some evidence to show that people under stress suffer more. You could consider a change in career and lifestyle.'

'But that's impossible. I'm in line for promotion in January. Believe me, it's not been an easy road in a male-dominated hierarchy. It's what I've worked for for years.'

Lauren nodded. 'In that case, I'd go for my first suggestion.'

Polly sat back and groaned, lifting her brows and nodding reluctantly.

There was nothing she could say, Lauren thought as she began to couch her referral after her patient had left, to persuade Polly to change jobs, and even if she did, who was to say it was a sensible suggestion anyway? Polly craved a challenge and had chosen to live her life for her career rather than a family. It was something that she had almost convinced herself she wanted in Africa— a career, a life of independence. . .without the man she loved. Except that now, of course, she was beginning to see how wrong she had been.

CHAPTER NINE

CHRISTMAS EVE fell on a Saturday.

Lauren had arranged a special surgery in the morning and Jessie had volunteered to come in for a couple of hours. Surprisingly, the list tailed off at eleven-thirty and Lauren let Jessie go to do the last of her shopping.

Waiting until midday, Lauren had decided she would close in another ten minutes, when Eliot walked in, his face set in a grim expression. He wore a camel coat and as he strode towards her his blue eyes glinted angrily. He faced her across her desk.

'Why didn't you come to me first, instead of going to Hugo?' he demanded. 'Do you hate me that much?'

'What are you talking—?' she began, only to be savagely cut off.

'The practice means that much to you, does it?'

Suddenly she realised he was referring to Hugo and her cheeks crimsoned.

'If I had known how desperate you were to see the back of me I'd have cleared out the minute you set foot in Gorsehall.'

She stared at him in disbelief. 'You don't mean that.'

'I do as a matter of fact,' he told her bitterly. 'I was a fool to think a professional partnership would ever work between us. As it is, you're welcome to the lot. You can have my share just as soon as you like, because quite frankly, Lauren, in the immortal words of a man with whom I now absolutely agree, "I don't give a damn".'

With that, he strode from the room without a backward glance and all she felt was the vibration of the door

123

shaking every nerve in her body as it slammed behind him.

When the phone rang next, it was Hugo. Lauren was still sitting at her desk, hurt and shaken, trying to work out what had caused the violent outburst.

'I'm sorry, my dear,' Hugo apologised flusteredly. 'Eliot phoned this morning and as I wasn't here, Amy took the call. She happened to say she would have mixed feelings this year as it would be our last Christmas at the practice.' He sighed heavily. 'And I've a feeling she may have given him the wrong impression. From the way she put it—quite innocently, but you know Amy— I think perhaps he may have thought you approached me about the partnership.'

Lauren sighed and sank back in her chair. She debated whether to tell Hugo what had just happened but she didn't want an upset between him and Amy on Christmas Eve of all times. Somehow she would have to try to resolve the misunderstanding herself. 'Don't worry,' she told Hugo quietly. 'I'll sort it out. Meanwhile have a happy holiday with the family.'

She could almost hear Hugo's intake of relieved breath. 'You too, Lauren. Let me know if I can be of help.'

But, of course, she wouldn't, would she? It was obvious, she thought as she replaced the phone, that Eliot had decided she had approached Hugo and asked about the partnership. Well, there was little she could do at the moment. And without much enthusiasm she began to try to think about the approaching holiday and her last-minute shopping.

The village was bustling with last-minute shoppers. She drove through it slowly, recognising a few faces and waving, and then parked at the general store to buy chocolates and fresh fruit and a cassette of carols to engender some Christmas spirit as she drove. When she went home the road to the cottage was congested, but at last she manoeuvred the Saab into the narrow lane, listening to 'O Come All Ye Faithful,' and drove slowly up it.

As she approached the house she narrowed her eyes at two figures which appeared to be sitting on the wooden bench by the front door under the bare vines of wisteria.

'Chrissie,' she breathed, 'and Eliot,' and she wound down the window as the car slowed.

'Hello, Dr Kent,' mumbled Chrissie.

The young girl sat huddled with Eliot's huge coat around her shoulders and Eliot sitting beside her in his suit, elbows on knees, and Lauren parked as quickly as she could and hurried over, shocked as she saw Chrissie's tear-swollen face.

'What's happened?' she gasped—a question which only made Chrissie burst into more tears.

Eliot hauled himself to his feet, took Lauren's arm and guided her back to the Saab. 'She's had a quarrel with her parents,' he explained in a weary voice. 'She says they've thrown her out and she's nowhere to go. This was the only place she could think of.'

'Here?' Lauren stared at the sobbing girl. 'But she can't stay here.'

'That's what I told her. I came home ten minutes ago to collect an overnight bag and I've been sitting here with her ever since, trying to persuade her it was just an upset she's had with her parents. I've offered to take her home, talk to her father.' He sighed and ran a hand through his hair. 'As you can see, I've got precisely nowhere.'

Lauren said quietly, 'Were you planning on leaving?'

'After what happened this morning I hardly think there's any point in me staying.'

It was hardly the moment for explanations, and even if she began to make them she wasn't sure he would believe her in his present mood.

'I'm on call, Eliot; I may have to go out at any time. Shouldn't we at least get her inside the house for the time being? She looks frozen.' She saw that he was considering this when another thought occurred to her. 'And what about David? Where is he in all this?'

'On tour apparently. She hasn't a clue when—or if she'll see him again.'

Lauren expelled a long breath. 'Let's all go in and warm up.'

He seemed to hesitate briefly and then shrugged and Lauren felt her shoulders droop with relief. If she could persuade him not to go for the moment then perhaps she could find the right time to begin to explain about the mistake Amy had made.

In the house it was warm and cosy but Chrissie stood shivering in Eliot's coat, tears still coming down her cheeks. 'What is your home number, Chrissie?' Lauren asked, and wrote it down as Chrissie reluctantly told her. She dialled it, then passed the receiver over.

'I can't!' whispered Chrissie.

'Oh, yes, you can,' said Lauren firmly. 'Tell your parents where you are, for a start.' And after a pause Chrissie took the phone and began to speak.

'I'll make the fire up,' Eliot said in a disgruntled voice, and went off to the drawing room. Lauren realised she might have a few minutes in hand whilst Chrissie was talking and she followed him, intending to broach the subject of Hugo, when she found him stacking the logs and complaining bitterly that there were no fire-lighters.

'I've some in the car,' she told him. 'I stopped at the store on my way home. I'll get them.'

'Don't bother.' The fire crackled magically under

his fingers. 'Looks as though it's caught.'

He stood up, wiping his hands on a once immaculately white handkerchief and stuffing it back in his pocket. When he looked at her he muttered, 'What are we supposed to do with the girl?'

'Lord only knows.' She stared at the overnight bag in the corner of the room. 'Eliot, about this morning—'

'You'll obviously feel happier without my presence in the house,' he interrupted her, with a shrug of his shoulders. 'If it will help I'll drop Chrissie back to her parents. Sounds like she might have made up with them.'

'Eliot, this is your home. . .'

'Much to my eternal regret,' he growled, gazing around him. 'The place has never been mine, not in spirit. I've been its caretaker, that's all. And after what I discovered today I don't feel there's any point in me staying on in the village. Buy the cottage back from me—it's going dirt cheap.'

'You're not serious?'

'Oh, yes, never more.'

Just then Chrissie ran back in floods of tears. 'D-Dad says I'm better of with you. He said you p-poked your nose into family affairs.'

It took enormous concentration to direct her attention back to Chrissie and for a moment Lauren was tempted to tell the girl to replace the receiver as she was in no mood for an argument over the phone on Christmas Eve. But when she saw Chrissie's swollen eyes and pathetic little figure she sighed and went out into the hall and tried to be as courteous as she could to the irate man.

She listened patiently for a full two minutes to a tirade and then, before she could speak, there came an ominous beep which meant he had slammed down the phone.

On her return she found that Eliot had begun to balance the burning logs into place and Chrissie had buried her head in the cushions of the sofa.

Lauren dragged off her coat and threw it on a chair. 'He's too angry to talk at the moment,' she said as calmly as she could. 'So, as I can't think what else to do, I suppose I had better dig out the turkey from the freezer.'

Chrissie jerked up her head, the sobbing mysteriously ceasing. 'You mean I can stay?'

'Just for tonight,' Lauren warned her firmly. 'After that, I'm afraid you will have to eat humble pie with your father, Chrissie. Hopefully, by then, his temper will have cooled and you can both talk sensibly to one another again.'

The girl nodded, but Lauren had her doubts.

'I'll be going, then,' Eliot said, and moved to retrieve his coat.

'Where?' Chrissie stared up at him. 'Surgery isn't open on Christmas Eve, is it?'

Eliot looked slightly fazed and Lauren found herself interrupting. 'No, it isn't.' She looked at Eliot with soft green eyes. 'Dr Powers meant he was going out to... er...deliver some last-minute cards. You look frozen, Chrissie. Why don't you run yourself a hot bath and look through my wardrobe for something warm to wear whilst I get organised down here?'

The idea of rifling Lauren's wardrobe obviously appealed and she jumped to her feet, running over to plant a kiss on Lauren's cheek. She turned briefly to Eliot, went scarlet, then shot upstairs.

'What was all that about?' asked Eliot, frowning at her.

'It is Christmas,' she said softly. 'We both seem almost to have forgotten the fact.'

She saw him hesitate and knew he was angry and hurt, just as she had been angry and hurt too, and he turned slowly away from her and walked to the window to stare out.

*   *   *

Chrissie looked a different girl by the evening.

She had bathed and washed her hair, which was a pretty, natural auburn underneath the orange dye, and she'd borrowed a pair of Lauren's jeans and a sweater. As Lauren was working in the kitchen, she left the tree to Chrissie, and Eliot absconded to the garden to cut yet more logs.

Lauren watched him from the kitchen. He wore only a T-shirt and jeans and his arms glistened with sweat as time and again he brought the axe down to split the huge logs. There was a mechanical saw, she knew, buried somewhere in the tool shed. She could only suppose he found the exercise therapeutic.

In the early evening Lauren was finally called out to a young child with a cough. The boy was seven and his mother was worried that it was whooping cough. But it was merely the excitement of Christmas playing on a dry throat and the prescription she gave was just for a soothing linctus. Whilst she was there, another call came on the mobile—Alan and Hilary Freen.

Angela, she discovered was fine. It was Hilary who was troubled, with sore patches in the mouth which had become very painful.

'Sorry to call you out,' she apologized, 'but I'm worried about passing on anything to Angela over Christmas.'

Lauren examined her mouth thoroughly. 'You have oral thrush, Hilary, and if you come in to the surgery next week I'll take a swab just to make sure. I'm going to prescribe some antifungal lozenges for now. There's a chemist open until nine in the village, if Alan can run up for you.'

'Oh, yes, thanks.' Hilary sighed as she looked down at a gurgling Angela in her tiny chair. 'I'm over-cautious about everything, I suppose, in view of what happened.'

'Well, avoid kissing her,' Lauren laughed softly,

'which will be an awful punishment, I know. She's so gorgeous!' Lauren washed and tidied away, then bent down to play with the baby.

'How's Eliot?' Hilary asked.

Lauren shrugged. 'Fine.'

'Is that all?' Hilary grinned in amusement.

Lauren felt her cheeks burn and tried changing the subject. But when she went to leave Hilary wished her and Eliot a happy Christmas—unable to disguise a teasing light in her eye.

Back at Gorsehall Cottage, Lauren found a surprise waiting for her.

'Go on!' Chrissie said as she walked into the hall, 'I went to the shop especially.'

Lauren stood under mistletoe, trapped by Chrissie's ingenuity. She had positioned the little bunch on a beam in the middle of the small room where now they stood, Eliot having just come down the stairs.

Lauren laughed dismissively and tried to walk away, but Eliot grabbed her wrist. 'Why not?' he asked, arching wry brows. 'Let bygones be bygones,' he whispered under his breath as he took her in his arms.

Chrissie giggled and Lauren flushed deeply. She was trapped whatever she did. Better get it over, she decided, standing stiffly, and when he brought his mouth down in a kiss that left nothing to the imagination she heard Chrissie's squeal of excitement as she watched them.

For once, Lauren blessed the phone when it shrilled, and Chrissie hurried over to answer it as Eliot still held her in his arms, refusing to let her go, with an amused smile spreading over his face that told her he was enjoying her embarrassment.

'How could you do that?' Lauren whispered, still in shock.

'Easily.' He shrugged and she felt his broad shoulders lift under her fingers. 'The girl clearly wanted something other than perpetual rowing in her life—I think we did rather well on the whole. . .considering.'

'You mean you kissed me for Chrissie's sake?'

'I could hardly refuse, could I? Wouldn't it have spoilt the happy family impression you're trying so hard to give?'

He finally let her go when Chrissie darted back to them. 'It was David,' she said excitedly. 'He's coming back from London tomorrow. He phoned home and my father told him I had moved into your house.'

'Did he indeed?' drawled Eliot, thrusting his hand through his hair.

'Oh, please don't be angry.' The girl was almost in tears again. 'I'm sorry I've involved you, I really am. But I just couldn't stay at home.'

Lauren found she was barely keeping her patience. 'We understand, Chrissie, but this is only deepening the rift between you and your family. They are bound to think we are taking sides.'

Chrissie pushed back the tears with an obvious effort. 'Dr Kent, I have a new family now. Me, David and the baby.'

Lauren felt a small lump in her throat at the girl's remark and she could not help but admire her courage, though the fact that her decision had implicated them seemed to have entirely missed Chrissie's reasoning.

Eliot glanced at his watch. 'Well, I'm all in. And Dr Kent might well have a call during the next few hours so I suggest we have a reasonably early night.'

Chrissie nodded and gave them both a shy smile. 'Thank you for having me here,' she said softly. 'And Merry Christmas.'

When Chrissie disappeared upstairs, Eliot sighed. 'Let's hope David produces one or two rabbits out of the hat tomorrow—assuming, of course, he turns up.'

Lauren nodded. 'She's a tough little thing. She does

really want the baby—and David.' Then she thought of her call earlier this evening. 'Talking of babies, Hilary wished us—er—you a happy Christmas. I said I would pass on the message.'

Lauren looked up at him, aware that he had moved towards her, and before she could say anything else he had taken her in his arms, and as her heart pounded he brought his lips slowly down on her open mouth.

Shakily she folded her arms around him, afraid to touch, afraid to let go of the flimsy control she had over herself. But her lids fluttered closed as he stroked back her dark hair and held her head between his hands as he kissed her. Images tormented her of how it once had been, of how unguarded her love had been. And yet, as he kissed her, the hurt seeped away to be replaced by the ache of her need for him which she had guarded so secretly over the last four years.

'For old times' sake,' he whispered as his tongue moved over her mouth and made her gasp for breath.

When she opened her eyes again, he was looking down at her, gently rubbing the pads of his thumbs across her cheekbones. Then he kissed her again, so deeply that she thought her legs might give way, so much pleasure filling her that she prayed the moment would go on for ever and she would never wake up to reality.

But in the next moment the phone rang yet again and Chrissie's feet could be heard thundering down the stairs. They broke apart quickly and Chrissie whipped past them to pick up the phone, obviously thinking it was David.

'It's for you, Dr Kent,' she said with a disappointed sigh, and gave the phone to Lauren before bolting upstairs again.

Lauren dragged herself to the phone and listened to the celebrations and the voice on the other end of the line.

*   *   *

Lauren woke on the sofa, where she had collapsed last night. Two false alarms and a premature birth had caused her to drop in exhaustion at around three in the morning.

What she did not recognise was the blanket that someone had pulled over her; her feet were tucked up minus shoes and there was a pillow behind her head. Eliot or Chrissie? She couldn't remember a thing, except feeling so tired that she must have completely blacked out when she'd come in.

Chrissie suddenly appeared, a tray of coffee in her hands.

'Chrissie, what time is it?' she asked in panic, struggling to sit up.

'Half-nine,' the girl told her, 'and no rush. Dr Powers told me to let you sleep after the night you had.'

Lauren blinked, vaguely aware it was Christmas morning. She checked her watch and gasped. 'So it is. Good heavens. I must—'

'Dr Powers has gone to a suspected appendix and taken the mobile phone; he said to tell you. And he said when you got angry about him not waking you, which you were bound to, to add that he's only taken calls so we can prepare him a proper Christmas dinner.'

Lauren stared at Chrissie wordlessly and then they both burst into laughter.

'He obviously knows you pretty well,' Chrissie giggled, handing over a cup of coffee.

Lauren sipped the drink thoughtfully and then looked at her young house guest. 'And what about you, Chrissie? Have you come to any decision about the baby?'

Chrissie's eyes filled with tears. 'Does that mean you think I'm wrong to have it?'

Lauren took her hand and tugged her down on the sofa. 'No, it doesn't. But it will be very important for you and David to tackle your problems. Where to live, for instance. How you will cope with his being away on tour. And working to a budget. Babies are expensive and they become more expensive as they grow older. Especially when the next one comes along.' She squeezed the small hand tighter. 'Which is what your father is thinking about right now. He wants a good life for you. He is afraid the responsibilities will be too much. He knows what it's like raising a family.'

'I love my dad,' Chrissie gulped. 'I felt I'd let him down when I became pregnant, but I love my baby and David too.'

Lauren nodded. 'Then, you have a head start. But you are going to have to let your family see you are serious.' Lauren smiled softly. 'Grandparents usually dote on their grandchildren and it's only a matter of time before the breach is healed, but meanwhile, give them something to go on.'

Chrissie blew her nose on a tissue and nodded. 'Thanks, Dr Kent. I'll try. The turkey's on, by the way. I hope you don't mind me messing around in the kitchen.'

'Absolutely not.' Lauren tossed aside the blanket. 'Give me ten minutes and I'll join you.'

And she was delighted when, a little more than ten minutes later, dressed in soft green and with her long dark hair flowing around her shoulders, she walked into the kitchen and found Chrissie already basting the bird.

'At least my mum made sure I knew how to cook.' Chrissie grinned shyly.

'And for that I shall be eternally grateful!' Lauren giggled. 'Now, point me in the right direction and see how much of a mess I can make with the vegetables.'

The table was set, the meat carved and the wine in the fridge when they heard Eliot's Rover pull up.

'Quickly,' Lauren said, 'put the cassette of carols on, Chrissie, whilst I turn the food on low.'

Chrissie flew away and Lauren snatched off her apron, smoothed her slim-fitting dress over her hips and took a last glance in the kitchen mirror. Huge green eyes which overshadowed her face, far too bright and excited. Cheeks flushed—the cooking, probably. Soft mouth curved in anticipation, hands and heart shaky. Lauren and Chrissie collided in the hall to a full choir of 'On The First Day of Christmas'.

'Ready?' Lauren mouthed. They each held a glass of bubbly in their hands; true, it was low alcohol, but it frothed and sparkled like real champagne.

Chrissie nodded and they pulled open the door. 'Merry Christmas!' they cried, and to their astonishment three people stood there, and each looked totally bewildered at the welcome.

'David!' gasped Chrissie, and, spilling her drink, rushed forward to throw herself into his arms.

'Mrs Viner!' exclaimed Lauren, and Eliot gently put a hand under the hesitant elbow, lifting dark brows at Lauren in silent communication. She understood all too well. The poor woman looked absolutely worn out and on the brink of tears.

'Come in, come in.' Lauren smiled. 'Merry Christmas, everyone!'

David and Chrissie disappeared into the front room and Shirley followed Lauren into the kitchen whilst Eliot dashed upstairs to change.

'Dr Kent,' she began helplessly, 'you didn't know Dr Powers was bringing me here, did you? He said you did, but I don't believe him.'

'Rubbish,' Lauren laughed softly. 'It's an open house this Christmas. Everyone is welcome, but especially you.'

The older woman pushed back her untidy hair. 'I just don't know what to say.' She forced back tears. 'Oh, dear, I look a mess, don't I?'

'Nothing a wash and brush-up won't cure, so have a drink and then slip up to my bedroom and freshen up.'

When Eliot came down a few minutes later, Lauren heard him on the staircase giving Shirley Viner directions to the bedroom. She listened to his footfall and smiled to herself as he hesitated at the front room but swiftly changed course to the kitchen.

She turned and arched a brow. 'Are they pleased to see each other?'

'Better put up a "Do Not Disturb" sign on the door for five minutes.' He smiled wryly. 'Or even a bit longer.'

He walked towards her and lent against the worktop. 'Sorry about Shirley Viner. I couldn't drive past the stables without wondering how she was. I remembered you'd mentioned the children had gone away. I found myself knocking on the door and when I saw her there alone. . .'

'I would have done the same thing,' she confessed, and lifted the spoon from the saucepan for him to test the warm liquid, her eyes meeting his as he moved closer.

He sipped, staring at her, running a smooth pink tongue around the edges of his lips. And as she dropped the spoon into the pan he drew her into his arms and kissed her.

'Happy Christmas,' he whispered huskily, his eyes touched with softness and yet a strange kind of intensity. Then he let his hands drop and, turning on his heel, he strode out of the kitchen, hands thrust deeply into pockets.

Considering the wretched night before, Lauren realized as the afternoon wore on that she might be lucky enough to get away with an uninterrupted afternoon. Not that it was too peaceful, not after the kiss in the kitchen which had left her totally confused.

She wanted to explain about Hugo and still hadn't found the time. It was as though they were having to put everything on hold personally and meanwhile act as if everything were quite normal, which, of course, it wasn't.

The meal was devoured by everyone and, totally satiated, they sat afterwards and listened to the Queen's speech.

It seemed a timeless message, Lauren thought. She had not listened to one since she was a girl and yet the underlying message was the same. Peace and unity. In Africa, there had been too little of either, and, glancing under her lashes at Chrissie and David curled on the sofa, she thought that their young lives up to now had been starved of both.

Not that she could make a claim to much more, she thought regretfully, turning her gaze to the man who had filled her thoughts for so long, even across oceans.

He sat a little away from her, his body relaxed and his dark head tilted to one side as he listened, and even though he seemed to be unaware of her gaze she felt the invisible pull towards him that would have singled him out of a room of many.

When the transmission came to an end, the front doorbell sounded and Tom Clancey appeared with a home-made chocolate yule log, which, apparently, he had been in the habit of making for Lauren's mother.

'Quite a party,' Eliot murmured beside her as they prepared yet more rounds of food and beverages.

'Tom seems to be taking Shirley's mind off her troubles,' Lauren said, and looked up into the hooded eyes.

'Not such a bad Christmas after all.'

She found her fingers encircled by his as they both reached for the same glass.

'Wh-what did you do last Christmas?' she stammered,

swallowing, asking the first thing that came into her mind and not bargaining for the answer.

He smiled softly, and against the backdrop of the noisy gathering he whispered, 'Your mother and I talked of old times and missed you.'

CHAPTER TEN

DAVID and Chrissie left at six to visit David's widowed mother and Tom Clancey offered to drive Shirley Viner back to the stables. Lauren helped him on with his coat in the hall. 'Thanks, Tom, for everything. It was good to have you here,' she said warmly.

'Oh, it's me who should thank you—you and Eliot— for making a lonely old man's Christmas a happy one.' He took her hands in his rough ones. 'If only your mother could have foreseen the way it turned out for you two. . . well, I'm sure she would never have acted so hastily all those years ago.'

Lauren gazed up at him in bewilderment. 'I'm sorry, Tom, you've lost me there.'

He frowned, his brow crinkling heavily. 'You mean. . .you don't know?'

'Know what?' Lauren asked hesitantly.

He squeezed her hands. 'Trust an old duffer like me to put his foot in it! Forget it, Lauren; I made a silly mistake, that's all. Got things confused.'

At that moment Shirley Viner appeared with Eliot, and Tom sallied into another one of his jokes, then before she could get around to talking to him again everyone filed outside and began saying goodbye. A few minutes later Lauren watched at the door as Tom's headlights disappeared down the lane.

'The day didn't go off so badly after all.' Eliot stretched beside her as she closed the door and leant against it with a sigh.

She smiled softly. 'Well, we couldn't spoil everyone else's fun, could we?'

'Even if we didn't have any ourselves?'

'We haven't argued either.'

He leant a hand against her head. 'No, we haven't.'

She wanted to talk about Hugo and yet something in his eyes made her keep silent, possibly because the way he was looking at her turned every bone in her body weak with longing.

'I think I had better go,' he said, and she put up her hand and laid it on his arm.

'Don't go. Not yet.'

He stood quite still and then reached out, slipping his hand around her waist, pulling her towards him. 'Do you know what you're asking?'

She nodded, slowly meeting his gaze.

'For old times' sake?' he whispered, drawing her close.

'For old times' sake,' she agreed, and knew that nothing could stop them now. Not even the thought that once he had used and hurt her so badly that she had thought she would never trust him again. She told herself that if she satisfied her body's craving this one time he would be out of her system once and for all. Then it wouldn't matter about misunderstandings or explanations or whether he understood about Hugo or not.

She felt his fingers working in her hair and she closed her eyes as he bent to kiss her, his hand sliding down to her bottom and drawing her in to his arousal.

'You're sure?' he muttered as she quivered in his arms. 'Just tonight?'

'Just tonight,' she repeated shakily. 'After all, it's Christmas.'

'So you keep telling me.' He reached out to snap off the hall light and pull the chain across the door behind her head as he took her hand and led her upstairs.

In her bedroom, he folded her into his arms and began to slide his fingers around the buttons of her dress, and he gazed at her with hooded eyes as she helped him with shaking fingers to undo the tiny pearls. By the time they'd reached the bed and she was lying on it, her dress had fallen to the floor and her lacy white bra was exposed as she stumbled with his shirt.

'Steady,' he whispered, gently pinning her arms above her head. 'Let me. . .' He lingered over her underwear, beginning to unwrap her at his leisure, peeling off the ivory stockings and suspenders with almost reverential care.

With her bra unfastened and breasts freed, he gazed in hungry appreciation at their ripeness, bringing his mouth to tease and suck the aching pink buds into peaks of sweet desire.

'You're more beautiful than ever, Lauren,' he whispered, his tongue moving over her lips and seeking her mouth with indescribable familiarity, and somehow her trembling fingers faltered to his clothing, tore away shirt and trousers, and she fluttered her hands over the forest of thick black chest hair, sliding them down to cup his heavy fullness.

She could not believe how much she had missed him. She remembered every muscle of his beautiful body and the way when he held her the sinews of his shoulders rippled and flexed inadvertently under her touch. No man had ever made her feel this way. She watched spellbound as his dark head travelled down to her abdomen, tongue flicking sensually over the flat, sensitive skin of her stomach, and she moaned softly, suffocating the little voice inside which called out that tomorrow she would be sorry.

But could she stop now? In turmoil, she knew that this was her last opportunity. . .tomorrow might hold the same disabling hurt and pain that the past had brought her. Could she risk all she had built since, just for one night of aching pleasure?

'Oh, Lauren,' he moaned, and then they were locked together. She cried aloud as he brought them both to a long-awaited release and he raggedly groaned her name again.

She held him as he sank away from her, his breath a ragged whisper.

'Just hold me,' she breathed shakily, and he wrapped her into his arms and she laid her head on his chest, listening to the even, powerful beat of his heart, and she knew that, whether it was madness or not, he had taken, once more, a part of herself—for ever.

Much later, they lay there, neither speaking. The cares of the outside world dawned suddenly and shockingly as she ran her hand over her eyes.

'Eliot?' she whispered, staring into the heavy-lidded blue eyes beside her. 'I'm on call, remember?'

He propped himself on an elbow and looked down at her with soulful eyes. 'The phone hasn't rung yet.'

She sank back, closing her eyes. 'Even so, I should be ready.'

'It's Christmas,' he murmured. 'Everyone in the village will be enjoying themselves too much tonight. Maybe in the morning. . .' He moved his leg across her to pin her down and she gave in to the sensation of his lips seeking to open her mouth as he pulled her into the proud jut of his hips and his hand provocatively ran down over her wriggling bottom, and for the next hour, as she was to remember afterwards, she broke every rule in the book.

The first call came minutes before a second call, at nine-thirty in the morning as she nestled in his arms, mind-blown with the pleasure he had given her over the long night. The phone rang beside them and he swung a long arm out to answer it.

She heard him mention Chrissie's name and she slipped from bed, wrapping her robe around her, and on automatic pilot was showering by the time he came in to find her.

'Was it Chrissie?' she asked, pushing back her wet hair, smothered in a huge white Turkish towel.

His dark hair was thrust untidily away from his face and the ragged look of a pirate made her heart skip a beat as she stood on the mat watching him.

'They've decided to stay with David's mother, who's offered them a room whilst she's pregnant,' he said, and she relaxed as he started to pull on a fresh sweater over his head. 'Then there was a second call, from a telephone box on the other side of Gorsehall. Someone's come off their motorbike.'

'I'm almost dressed,' she muttered, frantically beginning to fly around the room to look for clothes.

'I'm going, not you,' he told her, and came across and took hold of her. 'No arguments, Dr Kent,' he whispered, stroking her chin with a soft finger. 'The guy refuses to call an ambulance. I think he's probably worried about being breathalysed and there may be trouble.'

'But I'm on duty, Eliot, not you.'

'I'm not having you running about the countryside on a fool's errand,' he growled. 'Don't argue with me on this one, Lauren, please.'

And she didn't. She saw him off, then went back into the quiet house. She went slowly upstairs to her bedroom and ran her hand over the place where he had lain, remembering the way they had made love and wondering what would happen now. Last night had seemed so right and she had felt so desperate to be loved by him, but in the light of day. . .what would happen now?

She was in the kitchen and tidying the debris of the holiday, mostly to keep her mind occupied so that she didn't have to think, when he returned. Dressed in a sweater and casual navy trousers, he looked tall and slightly sombre, and followed her movements around the kitchen with a small frown. She stopped what she was doing and stared at him.

'Coffee?' she managed pathetically, and he nodded and she went to the percolator, sensing his movement to sit on one of the kitchen chairs.

Her heart was beating so fast that she made a deliberate effort to slow her actions. 'I'll get you some breakfast—'

'Lauren, sit down, will you?' he said, and caught her hand and pulled her down to sit beside him.

She smoothed down her denim shirt and jeans and avoided eye contact, but eventually she was forced to look up at him and they sat facing one another for a few seconds before he said abruptly, 'We need to talk.'

She nodded, clenching her hands under the table. 'What happened with the motorcyclist?'

'He'd come off on the bend going out of the village by the phone kiosk.' His voice was flat, as though the journey out had changed him somehow, given him time to think. 'My guess was a fractured ankle. As far as I could tell there was nothing else apart from a few cuts and bruises. He was well the worse for drink. When I tried to phone for an ambulance he took a lunge at me. Luckily, he was in too much pain to put up much of a fight and then a patrol car came by, saving me the trouble.'

'Was he from the village?' Lauren found herself deliberately procrastinating, wishing there were some way she could avoid the conversation she knew must come between them.

He shook his head. 'No, not as far as I could gather. Muttered something about finding our number in the directory, though God knows how he managed to through an alcoholic glaze.'

'Eliot, about. . .what happened. . .' she began, and realised she really didn't know what to say or how to express herself.

'We agreed it was. . .just last night—yes?' He lifted his head and stared at her, his eyes heavy with meaning.

She didn't know if it was a question or he was merely stating a fact, but, either way, the sinking sensation in her stomach made her realise he was waiting for an answer.

Limply, she nodded. She stared at him, recalling the desperation she had felt when he had abandoned her before, when she had trusted him so completely. If he had wanted her on a sudden impulse last night, she told herself, or because he couldn't tolerate the fact that she might be able to live without him. . .

Suddenly he stood up, bringing her thoughts to a shattering halt. 'I've an overnight bag packed—'

'I need to know, Eliot,' she interrupted, staring at him with wide green eyes, 'if. . .if last night you. . .'

'My God,' he muttered on an indrawn breath as he blinked hard, 'you think I made love to you because of the practice, don't you? That's what's going through your mind. You think I would take you to bed as the only way left to me to keep the practice.'

She met his gaze as he stared at her in disbelief. 'Eliot, four years ago, you hurt me so badly—'

'Which was why you went to Hugo to persuade him into turning over his share to you!'

'No, that's not the way it happened.' She swallowed the hurt of his accusation but she wasn't about to plead her innocence, and by the expression on his face he had already made up his mind about her guilt and was obviously going to listen to nothing she had to say.

'Well, I'll be damned.' He shook his head, staring at her with eyes full of bitter accusation. Then, making a snort of disgust, he swivelled angrily away from her, shoulders hunching angrily as he stopped at the kitchen door and turned back to face her. 'For the record,' he said, very slowly so that the anger in his voice seemed to make each word more powerful than the last, 'four years ago I did what I had to do. There was no way I was going to see you flunk those exams. That's the truth and if you can't accept you would have failed those finals because of us—because of my influence on you— then there really isn't very much more I can say.'

'So you admit you know how much you hurt me?' she persisted, aware she was like a dog with a bone who wouldn't let go.

'As I recall it, you couldn't take my assessment of your skills, because I wouldn't concur with the image you had of yourself as a surgeon.' He took a deep breath and lifted his shoulders. 'You could still have gone ahead and tried surgery and taken no damn notice of me at all if you'd wanted it so much.'

'How could I?' Her green eyes were suddenly moist with tears. 'After what you did to me I just felt I wanted to give up—'

'Giving up,' he said cutting her short, 'is a luxury no one can afford in medicine. And you learned that better without me than with me.'

She jumped to her feet, desperation making her voice shaky. 'I wanted you, Eliot, and a career. Lots of women marry and hold down a career. Why not me?'

He gazed at her for a long time and then shook his head. 'Because you were not "lots of women", Lauren. To me, you were a very special person who needed to find out what she was capable of—before she made a personal commitment which might not have been what she wanted, or needed, even if she thought so at the time.'

He walked slowly back into the kitchen and for one blissful moment she thought he was coming to take her in his arms, but instead he reached down and picked up his coat from the back of a chair, bringing his dark eyes up to her face. 'But that's all history,' he said bitterly as he strode back to the open door. 'And I think we both know it.'

Lauren sat at her desk on Friday afternoon thinking vaguely that she should leave for the cottage. A week had never passed so achingly slowly as the week between Christmas and New Year.

Eliot had taken his bag on Boxing Day and left the house and she had spent the rest of the holiday trying to stem the tears which kept on creeping down her cheeks at the most inopportune times such as when she was dealing with a patient and her mind suddenly broke away to think of him and of their last moments at the cottage together.

Jessie came in then, handing her the last batch of prescriptions to sign. 'Anything else, Dr Kent?'

Lauren looked up and smiled. 'No, Jessie. You might as well lock up now.' She flicked through the prescriptions, suddenly looking up hopefully as the receptionist went out. 'I suppose Dr Powers isn't still here, is he?'

Jessie shook her head. 'No, he left about an hour ago. Dr Lee and Dr Grant are in their rooms, though.'

'OK, thanks, Jessie.' Lauren wondered if it was as plain to the staff as it was to her that Eliot had avoided her all week. She had no idea where he had gone and she couldn't bring herself to ask Hugo or Charles. Was he with Caroline Peters? she wondered miserably.

'Don't look so glum.'

Lauren jumped at the voice. 'Charles.' She swallowed hard, standing up to face him. 'I was miles away. Have you finished?'

'For the entire weekend,' he boasted amiably, coming to perch a thigh on her desk. 'Hugo is covering the on-call and I believe you and Eliot are finished this evening, aren't you?'

She nodded. 'Well, enjoy your celebrations—you will be celebrating, I take it?'

'I've nothing special in mind. . .' He grinned teasingly. 'How do you fancy celebrating with me? We could storm the West End together. See a few shows. Overdose on forbidden fruit.'

She smiled. 'What a pity. I just happen to have a house to clean and a freezer to fill.'

'Yes.' He nodded with an exaggerated sigh, rubbing his chin. 'I can see it must be a deadly choice for you, but. . .' he shrugged, standing up and gesturing dramatically '. . .I know when it comes to filling freezers and washing hair a guy is beaten hands down. Happy New Year anyway,' he chuckled, and bent to kiss her just as Eliot walked into the room.

Lauren found herself going pink although the kiss had been innocent enough. 'I thought you were gone,' she mumbled, and stood up.

'I was. I came back to collect something I'd left in my room.' He glanced at the younger doctor. 'And I thought I'd wish you all the best for New Year, Charles.'

With a rueful grin at Lauren, Charles shook Eliot's hand and thanked him, then, a smile plastered all over his face, left rather smartly.

'I obviously interrupted,' Eliot said in a distant voice.

'No, not at all.' Lauren stiffened, aware of the accusation in the blue eyes and the unintentional coolness in her own voice. 'What can I do for you?'

'It's more a question of what I can do for you.' He threw a file he had been holding onto her desk. 'A New Year's present—one you've been waiting for, I dare say—details of when I shall be leaving and where I shall be going.' He paused, his mouth tightening as she picked up the folder. 'And as far as my share in the practice goes

I've had a word with Ken Howard. He's recommended a colleague who will handle the negotiations for me—and the sale of the cottage.'

Lauren stared at him wildly. 'Eliot, I don't know what to say. Can you wait a second——?'

He turned at the door, shrugging coldly. 'Wait for what? A royal pardon for crimes committed four years ago?' He laughed hollowly. 'No, thanks. I think I'd rather take my chances elsewhere.'

When she arrived home, she knew at once he had been in the cottage. She could smell him, sense him. . .every stitch of clothing had gone. Every sweater, shirt, shoe and personal effect. Only the scent of his cologne was left hanging in the air and there was the incongruous sight of his key on the kitchen table.

She saved opening Eliot's folder until she was more composed and she'd made herself an omelette and managed, although she hadn't been hungry, to get it down her with several cups of strong tea. Food, however, made no difference to the outcome of her reading the contents of the folder. Sitting in front of the fire that night, she still felt a leaden weight in her stomach as she opened the file and read.

Eliot intended to leave the practice in March. He had written to Hugo and enclosed a copy for her. It stated briefly the simple facts. Professor Tomlinson had left a practice in Oxford and Eliot intended to improve and modernise it, as he had done with the Village Surgery. The name of Ken Howard's colleague was given as negotiator for the financial and legal settlements and he thanked Lauren, Hugo and Charles for the support he had received since joining the practice.

Lauren realised she couldn't read on. She laid down the folder and ignored the other documents, which she had seen were to do with the sale of Gorsehall Cottage to her. The sum printed in small black letters at the foot of the covering page was ridiculously low.

It was some while before she allowed herself to continue. She sat in a kind of numbness, until, realising she must get it over, she turned her attention to the blue airmail letter which had arrived by late post this morning.

Redirected by the post office, it had lain for months in a Mombasa sorting department and had at least half a dozen different addresses printed and crossed out on the front, the date of posting, horrendously, five months previously.

In her mother's bold, clear handwriting it read.

Darling Lauren,

I hope all is well, though I have not heard from you for several months. I credit this to the post, as your last two letters from East Africa arrived almost at the same time. I shall be brief, darling.

Just after you went away, I began to have a few minor health problems, mostly angina. However, I'm feeling much better now and am looking forward to seeing you in the spring and learning firsthand of your work.

There is much I have to tell you. The practice is, as I always hoped, flourishing now. My only wish is that I could explain Eliot's presence in our lives more fully. But this I think must come from Eliot himself. Whilst you were at medical school, I made an unforgivable intrusion in your lives. I hope, in some way, I have made reparation for this.

Please know that everything I have ever done has been solely with your best interests at heart. I know general practice would never have filled the need you have in medicine. But still I have hoped. Your father began the Village Surgery and I continued here. Therefore, if ever I have hoped you would show an

interest, it was purely for selfish reasons. Good luck,
my darling, in all you do, whatever it may be. Until
we meet again, God bless you, Lauren.

Love and thoughts, as always, Mother.

Lauren read and reread it. The minutes of the evening
ticked away as she sat there in darkness. She had been
staring at the letter in the light of the open fire. What
had her mother meant by intrusion in her life? Lauren
wiped her cheek and took a deep breath. She supposed
that, unless she asked Eliot, she would never know.

She folded the letter and tucked it safely into her bag.

It was the third week of February when Lauren realised
she had missed her period. If she was painfully honest
with herself, she'd missed two, coming on three, since,
when she checked in her diary, she discovered that she
had had her last period in late November.

The realisation brought with it a clammy perspiration
and the usual nausea which had crept over her in the
early mornings for the last week. Then Polly Sharp came
in to see her and Lauren slipped away her diary, looking
up to see an equally white face. Sinking into the chair,
Polly unbuttoned the rather shabby jacket she wore, so
much in contrast with the sophisticated Polly whom
Lauren had first known.

'This came this morning,' she said, laying a crumpled
letter on the desk. 'As you can see, I chucked it away,
but now I've had second thoughts.'

Lauren picked it up and saw it gave an admission date
to the London clinic to which she had referred her. 'It's
good news, Polly. You're accepting, I take it?'

Polly shrugged. 'I don't seem to have any choice.'
Then a fraction more hopefully, she added, 'If I do, they
indicate a four-week course. Can you sign me off sick
from work for a month? I'd need a certificate.'

Lauren nodded. 'I think it could be arranged, yes.'

'And pills. I desperately need pills.'

Lauren hesitated, tapped a few digits on her keyboard and frowned at the screen. 'I prescribed two months' supply of painkillers for you at Christmas, Polly. You should still have at least a week's supply left.'

Polly produced the empty bottle from her bag. 'I doubled the dose after Christmas. In the night I was woken up by terrible pain; I just couldn't cope.' She laid a hand on her abdomen. 'I began to dread going to sleep. So in the end I just took more.'

'You should have seen me first, Polly.'

She nodded slowly. 'To be honest I'm sick to death of coming to this place. No offence, but it's just not my scene.'

Lauren was well aware that for many patients the surgery could become either a watering hole in times of trouble or, sadly, a horror, and it was clear that Polly subscribed to the latter view. 'Look, I'm going to give you seven days' supply. If you are going into the clinic on the nineteenth then the doctors there will assess you for more.'

Polly nodded reluctantly, slumping back in her chair as Lauren computed the prescription and wrote the sickness certificate. When this was done, Lauren walked with her to the door and touched her shoulder gently. 'Have you someone to travel up with you?'

'Yes, a friend from work, thanks.'

'You know you're doing the right thing, don't you?'

Her patient laughed shallowly. 'I haven't an earthly what I'm doing. I just don't know myself any more— but I'll take your word for it. To be honest, I never realised I was such a negative thinker.'

'You're not,' Lauren disagreed firmly. 'Stop being so hard on yourself.'

After a little pep talk, when Polly had left, Lauren

wished she could feel confident of her judgement. The
clinic treatment, which was relatively new and which
she had only known of from high recommendations by
colleagues at St Margaret's, worked for some people,
not for others. She rifled her drawer and brought out a
file, studying the latest figures she had received from
the clinic concerning IBS, multiple sclerosis, chronic
musculoskeletal pain, limb amputation and chronic
fatigue syndrome. They showed in the majority improve-
ments in mobility, energy levels and well-being—all
achieved without medication.

Would Polly respond? she wondered. Out of the thirty
patients documented who'd started the course on painkillers, only one fifth had still needed them on discharge.
Hopeful results. But Polly was unusually depressed and
becoming reliant on the pills.

Lauren turned back to her desk and then changed her
mind and hurried along to the cloakroom. She felt very
sick and her slowly growing fear was beginning to
crystalise into certainty. This was not a flu bug, or the
malaria, but something she just could not believe was
happening.

She suddenly burst into tears, another symptom which
seemed to follow the sickness, and for the next ten
minutes sheltered in the little washroom, trying to make
sense of what was happening to her.

The week did not drag its feet.

She heard no more from Polly so she assumed she
had admitted herself to the clinic, and there was a fresh
outbreak of viral problems to contend with; in the meantime she was on call over the weekend, which gave
her an almost sleepless Sunday night as the phone rang
continually.

She was in the process of trying to quell the rising
sickness at nine o'clock on Monday morning when the

phone rang. 'Dr Powers on line two for you, Dr Kent,' said Robin.

'Put him through,' Lauren mumbled, and took a breath, telling herself she wasn't nauseated and was as right as rain.

'Lauren, I've just left Tom Clancey,' he said in the same polite, distant tone he had been using since Christmas. 'Early this morning he had a pretty severe angina attack. I want to admit him, but the old devil won't have it.'

'And you'd like me to call to see what I can do?'

'That's the general idea, yes.'

'OK, I'll call, but I don't promise to get results. How is he now?'

'Pretending nothing has happened, as usual. And there's just one more thing—our nurse has just gone home with flu, which leaves me without any help for a small op, a leg mole I'm going to excise for Chrissie Searle's younger brother. In about a quarter of an hour's time?'

'I'll see my last patient and I'll be in,' Lauren said as she glanced at her list which had almost come to an end.

She put down the phone and though the room began to swim in front of her she beat the urge to heave and went to call her last patient. As luck would have it, she had cancelled and Lauren told the girls at Reception she would be in the small ops room with Eliot if they wanted her.

But just as she decided to go in there another surge of sickness made her change her mind. This really was ridiculous and yet, she realised, she was hardly in any condition to help Eliot for the moment. On the spur of the moment she decided to run up the flight of stairs to the first floor to the cloakroom there and as she entered the room she was dismayed to find two of the cleaners putting away their equipment in the cupboard.

'Morning, Dr Kent,' one of the women said. 'Do you want to come in here? We're almost finished.'

'Er. . .no, it's all right, thanks,' she mumbled, and shot out again. There was only one place left where she could feel ill in privacy and that was the small emergency room on the top floor which was reserved for staff only.

It was a plain white room with blinds, a single bed and an adjoining toilet and shower. In the old days it had been used as a stock room, crammed with boxes of prescription pads, paper, surgical accessories and whatever else her mother hadn't been able to contain downstairs.

She hurried to the cloakroom, where she waited for her tummy either to erupt or settle. The feeling was as though she was on a permanent helter-skelter, and she only wished she could get off it. For a few moments she thought she was going to vomit as she had done for the past week, but slowly, as she took deep breaths and began to contain herself, the feeling wore off.

Having splashed her face with water in the little basin, she dabbed her skin with the paper towel and went back to the bed and sat on the edge of it. Well, there could be no doubt, she realised. She would make her own test later on, but it was really not necessary.

Could it really be true? she wondered, licking her dry lips.

And how was she going to tell Eliot? If she told him. She worried away at the prospect for a moment and then caught sight of his overnight bag pushed unceremoniously into the corner of the room. He must have left it there away from prying eyes and then the truth hit her again. He wasn't returning to Gorsehall cottage and he had no intention of doing so and, whatever the repercussions of their one night of making love, he had left the house for good, and by telling him she was pregnant surely she would only be holding a gun to his head?

Did she want the father of her child to return to her under those circumstances?

She sat very still, trying to think of how she would tell him, but she could not imagine that after what had happened between them there could be any response but dismay.

Wearily, she rose to her feet, took a breath and made her way downstairs. At least the nausea seemed to have abated for the moment although she still felt shaky. In the small ops room, she found herself alone and began to wash at the sink and dress in one of the sterile gowns that the nurse had left out.

Eliot soon joined her with his patient, a very nervous Brian Searle, who removed his trousers and climbed on the bench. After a few moments, Eliot began to explain what he was about to do in such a way that she could see, Brian visibly relaxed and she managed to freeze the area without his seeming to notice.

'What are the chances of it being skin cancer?' Brian asked worriedly as Lauren handed Eliot the tiny scalpel and watched him skilfully begin to lift the blemish.

'Very small,' Eliot replied. 'I'll send what I remove to histology, that is for analysis of the sample, but only as a precautionary measure. With you having knocked it and made it bleed, it was safer to take it out, but as far as I can see it looks very inoffensive.'

In no time at all it was done, the sample set aside for labelling and four very neat stitches put in.

'Come in at the end of next week to have those stitches removed and we should have the results by then,' Eliot told him.

'How are Chrissie and David?' Lauren ventured to ask as she dressed the small wound, and helped him off the bench.

'Oh, we see quite a bit of them now.' He grinned

shyly. 'Mum's knitting things for the baby and Dad's making a play-pen.'

Lauren shot a glance at Eliot and he smiled and when the boy had gone he murmured drily, 'Perhaps you're right about a happy ending.'

She paused in her disrobing. 'For Chrissie and David. . .yes, I think so.' And when he frowned at her less than enthusiastic answer she quickly asked him, 'Is there anything else in the way of small ops today?'

He shook his head, peeling off his gloves and gown. 'Nothing booked luckily. Thanks for that. I'll get it off to histology straight away.' His tone was abrupt but he came to stand beside her and for a moment she longed to be drawn into his arms and tell him everything, have the same courage Chrissie had shown when it had seemed the world was against her. But the moment passed as the door opened and he was beckoned by one of the reception girls.

Alone in the room, she stood still, staring out of the window, then she could bear her thoughts no longer and hurried back to her own room to fetch her coat and bag. She needed some fresh air and as she had no appointments left she would take an early lunch and walk through the village to take her mind off her worries.

As she slipped out the back way and headed across the car park, she heard her name being called and looked up to see Caroline Peters hurrying towards her.

'Dr Kent, I'm so glad I caught you before you left,' she called breathlessly, her blonde hair lifted by the breeze. Lauren managed to smile but before she could say anything Caroline hurried on. 'It's my last day with Amroco, didn't you know?'

'No. I had no idea. Have you something else lined up?'

Caroline smiled mysteriously. 'Yes, possibly. A move to Oxford, I think.'

Lauren felt the impact in her chest as she stared at the

girl. 'Oxford?' she repeated stupidly, and listened to the enthusiastic description of the new drugs company with whom Caroline hoped to be employed.

When at last they said goodbye, Lauren went to her car and unlocked it and sat down in the driver's seat as a light film of perspiration covered her forehead. Why had Caroline's moving to Oxford come as such a shock to her? Surely she should have realised that Caroline would not want to remain in the south if Eliot was moving to Oxford?

She put her hands to her stomach and swallowed, thinking what a fool she was. Only moments ago she had almost blurted out to Eliot that she was pregnant.

CHAPTER ELEVEN

'Is THERE anything I can say to persuade you to go in for a check, Tom?' Lauren sat in the cosy room which smelt of wood, two honey Labradors snoozing at her feet.

Tom Clancey laughed. 'You haven't an earthly, young lady.'

'What shall I do with you, you old rogue?'

He gave her a sidelong glance from the armchair. 'Stop that man of yours before he goes off and does something he regrets,' he said quite seriously.

'He's not my man, Tom,' she began, pushing her stethoscope quickly back in her bag, avoiding his eyes.

'Fiddlesticks,' he contradicted her gently. 'What's up, lass?'

She sighed, biting down on her lip. 'He's decided to move to another practice and build it up. That's about it, really.' She took out her handkerchief and sniffed and pulled back her shoulders.

'He's just built this one up,' the old man said. ''Sides, there's you to stay for now.'

Lauren shook her head, unable to meet his gaze. 'It's over between us, Tom. You might as well know—someone else from the practice is moving with him.' She hurried on as he opened his mouth. 'Now, for the last time, will you please let me admit you for a check-up?'

He stood up and warmed his backside against the fire, digging his hands thoughtfully into his trouser pockets. 'Lauren, if I went tomorrow I would die a happy man. I've lived a long and busy life. I haven't any regrets except one—I couldn't persuade your mother to get hitched, that's all.' He smiled as Lauren's face softened. 'And, talking of your mother, ask that young whipper-snapper for the whole story. He'll know what I mean.'

'Eliot?' She shook her head. 'No, I don't think that would be a good idea, Tom.'

'You love him, don't you?'

Lauren lifted her eyes and could not lie. She nodded, bringing out her handkerchief and giving a good blow this time.

Tom came to her and put an arm around her shoulders. 'A piece of advice from an old man who regrets having missed his chances. Talk to him. Tell him what's on your mind. Because there's something, isn't there?'

She found herself mumbling, 'Yes.'

And he squeezed her shoulder and muttered a laconic, 'Thought so.' Then he walked with her to the car and, before she climbed in, he held her arm. 'Promise?'

'I'll think about it.'

He held the car door and smiled wryly. 'Not good enough.'

Finally she gave in and made her promise, but it was the last promise on earth she felt like keeping as she drove away.

Point one. Eliot had been seeing Caroline before she'd come back on the scene last year. Which meant that she was the interloper, not Caroline. Point two. The fact Eliot had made love to her—whilst seeing Caroline—could be called two-timing. But then, in a way, she understood it. What had come over them at Christmas had been just too powerful for either of them to explain satisfactorily. Physical satisfaction, the slaking of a desire four years old which had been cruelly curtailed, loneliness, or God knew what else, it hadn't stopped them that night.

Point three, since then, of course, she had seen the look in Caroline's eye when the other woman had talked of Eliot and nothing could alter the fact that Caroline's moving to Oxford was because of their relationship.

Lauren drove away from Tom Clancey's, returned to a deserted surgery and left a note for Eliot on his desk. She paused reflectively as she laid it there, wondering if she should add anything to its clinical efficiency. They had written copious notes since Christmas—polite, to-the-point memos, so that neither of them would have to face the other.

All she had written was that there was no hope of her changing Tom's mind and she had done what she could but he still remained adamant in his refusal of a check-up. Deciding it was enough, she locked up, climbed back in the Saab and firmly put the promise she had made to the old man at the back of her mind as she drove home to nurse the nausea which still wretchedly persisted.

A few days later, there was snow.

It came first in a soft flutter, almost without anyone knowing. Then increasingly the sky dulled to a stone-grey, a wind whipping into a small frenzy over the tops of the trees of the Forest. Lauren stopped the Saab twice on the way to work in the morning, allowing ponies to cross the lane into the shelter of the village. Here they would find walls to lean against or an open barn door and very likely the odd bale of hay left out by a garden gate. When she nosed the Saab onwards through the main street, Gorsehall was busily sweeping its front doorsteps and shovelling pathways to the shops.

The practice looked like a Dickensian Christmas card, with just the faintest glimmer of a brass plaque outside the front door to distinguish it. All else was covered in a flawless white coat.

'You managed it, then?' Jane asked as Lauren gingerly stepped in and brushed the snow from her jacket.

'I probably would have done better with skis,' Lauren protested. 'How about everyone else?'

Jane nodded to the name-plates. 'Dr Grant rang to say he'll be here in about an hour. And Dr Lee has already gone on urgent calls. As for appointments, we've about half who have cancelled. Which means you'll probably be able to take a half-day.'

Lauren sighed. 'Don't tempt me.' She was almost to her room before she turned back and asked after Eliot.

'No word yet.' Jane shrugged. 'His surgery's at eleven, but three have cancelled already.'

In her room, Lauren shrugged off her coat, hung it up and smoothed down the fine amber wool dress. In the mirror she tidied her hair and picked a few flakes from its dark thickness. Her cheeks were stinging with the cold and were pink for a change and a pair of troubled green eyes gazed back at her thoughtfully.

She ran her hands over her flat stomach. Nothing showing yet, of course. Still, at least she had confirmed the pregnancy. Somewhere in there was the tiny embryo, the spark of life that she and Eliot had created on their one night together. It was an irony she could hardly believe. One night. And neither of them had thought of protection—they had been too whipped away by their desire. . .

She shivered and sat down at her desk, rubbing her arms to get warm. At least the sickness had abated before she had left the cottage, but she had the most amazing impulse to eat strawberries.

She glanced at her watch. Not usual for Eliot to be in late. Since Christmas he had arrived for work before everyone, and that included Jane who was often at the practice by seven-thirty. Still, the snow was thickening—and besides, where did Caroline live? She had never found out, never had the courage to ask either of the girls in case they might wonder why. The only phone

number in connection with Caroline was Amroco
Pharmaceuticals.

Just then the intercom sounded and Robin's voice
came over. 'Dr Kent, Mrs Shirley Viner is here though
she hasn't an appointment. Have you a few spare
moments? You've no one waiting.'

'Yes, please send her in,' Lauren agreed quickly. She
had been wondering how the Viners were and if there
had been any news. But she had been so preoccupied
with her own troubles since Christmas that she hadn't
got around to calling.

Shirley Viner came in, her short dark hair in a neat
cut and her eyes looking bright and eager. Lauren was so
surprised that she almost gasped out her good morning.

'Dr Kent, thank you for seeing me,' Shirley said
breathlessly. 'I called your home but you must have left.'

'Because of the snow I made an early start this morning.' Lauren gestured to the chair. 'You're looking so
much better. How are you?'

'You mean, you don't know?' she asked in surprise
as she sat down. 'Dr Powers didn't tell you?'

Lauren shook her head. 'Tell me what?'

'Well, it's just that on the way home from your house
at Christmas Tom Clancey said he'd like to have a look
around the stables. I could hardly believe my ears when
he made me a proposition. He says he's been looking
for an investment for the future in the Forest and says
he wants to retire, because lately his garage and his
recovery service have been a bit too much for him, and
that if I could find George and bring him back somehow,
he'd let us stay on as managers.'

Lauren stared at her in amazement. 'But that's
wonderful,' she gasped, thinking she should have known
that Tom was up to something.

'And that's not all,' Shirley Viner went on, bursting
to tell her now. 'Dr Powers rang me last night. He said

he'd traced George and he's been staying on a farm somewhere near Winchester of all places. Did I want him to drive up and check, see if there was anything he could do.'

Lauren tried to digest the news and saw that the poor woman was almost in tears with the excitement of it all. 'Did you tell Dr Powers about Tom's offer? she asked.

'Oh, yes, of course. That's why I'm here; I wondered if there was any news?'

Lauren shook her head. 'Not as far as I know. . .but then some of the roads are blocked out of town. He may have got held up.'

Ten minutes later, as she closed the door on her departing patient, the phone rang. 'Winchester General,' Jessie said, and then a brisk voice announced that it was Sister Stewart speaking.

'Dr Powers was involved in a road-traffic accident last night,' she told Lauren. 'He sustained concussion and a fracture to his arm—amongst other things.'

When Lauren had got over the initial shock, she told the sister who she was and that she would drive up immediately if the roads were clear.

'That would be helpful,' answered the voice drily, 'because he is threatening to discharge himself and quite honestly is making life very difficult in the process.'

'Tell him,' Lauren said firmly, 'if he sets one foot out of the hospital he will have to answer to me. I think you'll find that will do the job, Sister Stewart.'

Not only did Lauren check the roads with the police, but she arranged with Jessie to transfer her remaining patients to Hugo and Charles and to do the same with Eliot's remaining list.

'Poor Dr Powers,' gasped Jane when Lauren explained what had happened. 'We hadn't an earthly he was up Winchester way. Are you sure you should drive? Why not let one of the men go?'

'Because, knowing Eliot, he would persuade Hugo or Charles to bring him back instantly.'

'And he won't get around you quite so easily, is that it?' murmured Jane with a rueful grin.

'Absolutely not.'

Of course, when she was nosing the Saab out of the car park and driving carefully through the village, it was perfectly clear she had jumped the gun. Presumably Eliot could not drive himself, so how had he proposed to return—by taxi, or train? Madness in the condition he was in. So why had she offered to drive up in this unholy weather?

Lauren decided not to think about it and concentrated on the slippery road ahead. The worst bit was from Gorsehall to Cadnam. Then when she joined the round-about and the busy main thoroughfare there was no problem at all, as the police had advised her. The snow had changed to a fine, transparent drizzle and the gutters were full of black sludge. She reached her destination in an hour and ten minutes, in fact and parked at the back of the hospital, buying grapes and fruit juice in the hospital shop.

She found the wards busy with the midday meals being served. Nevertheless, she went straight to Orthopaedics, was directed to the second floor and then stood at the ward entrance in silent contemplation of the battle-scarred but familiar figure sitting stiffly in a bedside chair.

She tried not to think about how he made her feel. And indeed, as she made herself put one foot in front of the other, she refused to admit to the overpowering urge to run and throw her arms around him. Instead she dodged the lunch trolley and came to an abrupt halt at the foot of the bed.

A pair of dark eyes slowly lifted themselves—dark because they were blue and purple and bruised—and above the inky smudges there was white gauze taped, highlighting the half-dozen abrasions over his face.

He gave her a twisted smile with a swollen top lip. 'No visitors until two,' he muttered and prised himself up and out of the chair. 'But I suppose you would count as an exception.'

She moved towards him, unsure as to what to do, but deciding to avoid the arm cast and sling, she leant across and brushed a kiss on his cheek. 'You look awful,' she mumbled, trying to steady her voice.

'Thanks,' he grunted. 'Just what I needed, a little supportive flattery.'

'Oh, Eliot,' she groaned, and sunk into a chair. 'I'm sorry. You're just a bit of a shock to the system, that's all.'

He frowned at the grapes she pushed into his lap. 'I'm not staying long enough to eat those things. That's what you've come for, I take it—to drive me home?'

'Like that?'

He glared at the sling. 'Oh, this is nothing. The radius is fractured near the wrist. I've got one of those light-weight resin things instead of plaster. Can't abide plaster.'

'I'll bet Casualty loved you,' she sighed. 'What else?'

'Nothing particularly.'

She lifted her brows. 'Only concussion and God knows what else by the look of your posture.'

'Hospitals are terrible places,' he complained, sitting upright and flinching.

'And doctors make terrible patients.'

'I can see I'm not going to get much sympathy. A man decides to do a good turn, gets driven into, cata-pulted into a ditch and has to be cut free from a wreck and then is insulted.'

She grinned. 'I heard about your mission of mercy from Shirley Viner. In the circumstances, it would have been sensible to let someone know where you were leaping off to, don't you think?'

He waved this aside and, lowering his voice, demanded, 'When are you going to get me out of here?'

'As soon as the doctor discharges you. You know the ropes, Dr Powers.' Just then a tray landed on his bedside table, bearing a plate with a covered top and a knife and fork. 'I think I'd better disappear whilst you eat,' she decided quickly.

'Wait. . .' he reached out and grabbed her with his good hand, which seemingly had not lost any of its power as it locked around her wrist. 'Meet me in the day room in half an hour. We'll be able to talk in peace.'

'Can you walk there?'

'Of course I can walk. There's nothing wrong with my legs.'

With a shudder of remembrance of the last time she had seen them, nakedly parading across her bedroom, she was inclined to agree. 'Eat up. It'll do you good,' she muttered, and quickly dodged the quizzical frown he gave her.

She took herself to the cafeteria, ordered a large black coffee and a Danish pastry. As she sat and toyed with it, the resounding question was why was she here and not the obvious choice, Caroline? Why hadn't she thought to contact Caroline through Amroco instead of dashing up here like a lunatic?

After drinking her coffee and taking a few bites of the pastry she hurried to repair the damage to her hair and make-up in the cloakroom, taking off her coat. Her dark hair, having been freshly washed this morning, flew out from her head as she brushed it. Green eyes were. . . a preoccupied green, she thought critically, adding a touch of mascara. Again she glanced at herself in the full-length mirror and ran her hands over her abdomen.

She would be about eight weeks—no, nine. The

embryo would be evolving into foetus; she would have developed her tiny heart, and her limbs would have become mysterious little buds, beginning the tiny impression of fingers and toes, and her features, though blunt, would be shadowing into eyes and ears and mouth.

Her. . .? Lauren let out a small gasp of surprise. Somehow she knew she was carrying a girl. Caught in the astonishing sensation of the maternal rapport she was already having with her baby, Lauren sat for a moment and covered the place where the child resided with her fingers.

She wanted this baby more than anything else in the world. In comparison with how she felt now paled all her previous emotions. She knew just how Chrissie had felt, poor kid. And she knew, too, that the pivotal point of her existence was to protect and love this child. . . even if, God help her, she remained in a single state to do it.

She got up on shaky legs and tried not to think about Eliot. But it is Eliot's child, a voice which would not be squashed told her, and as she walked slowly back to the ward it continued to disturb her. A right to life. . .a right to know your parents. . .a God-given right. . .

And five minutes later, when her eyes alighted on the lone figure hunched in the chair in the day room, they turned a dark, shimmering green, filled with tenderness.

'Hello,' she said, and sat down.

'Find yourself a coffee?' he asked, and tried to smile.

'Yes, thanks.'

They were silent for a moment and then both began to speak at once.

'I found George,' he told her with a twinkle in his eye. 'The address having materialized with the help of the health department's computer, I discovered he is living with a farmer—an old friend apparently. After the shock of finding me on the doorstep he eventually let me in. Says he's ashamed of leaving his family, yet he didn't know what else to do.'

'Didn't he realise how worried Shirley and the kids have been?'

'Oh, he's been worried all right. But he thinks he's cracking up—and even when I told him the test results he couldn't seem to take it in. I spent a couple of hours trying to persuade him to come back with me, outlining Tom's offer as well. But it was all a bit too much for him, I think.' He lifted dark brows, the only things which seemed to be working properly on his face. 'Lucky he didn't, though, because as I turned out from the farm a car shot over the crossroads and. . .well, you know the rest.' He looked at her with resignation. 'All I want to do now is get out of here.'

She sighed, quiet for a moment. 'You know, if we were in each other's shoes you would be telling me to stay where I was for my own good.'

He gave a small sigh and winced as he shrugged. 'I suppose you're right. I didn't expect you to come all this way. . .I thought Hugo or Charles. . .'

She smiled. 'Sister Stewart made it quite plain you found the idea of staying here most disagreeable.'

He crooked an eyebrow at her. 'I suppose I did go off the deep end a bit.'

She grinned at him. 'A bit?'

'Well, what's a man supposed to do when he's carted in like a sack of potatoes—'

'The same as all your patients,' she retorted swiftly. 'Take your medicine and don't complain.'

He mumbled something under his breath and she gazed into the purply blue eyes crowned with a wodge of white gauze, at the same time moving her fingers over her stomach, and she found herself wanting to tell him. This was their baby she was carrying. They had made her together; they had conceived a life. And even if she did summon enough courage to tell him this was probably the last place on earth he would want to hear it.

'I think we'd better get back,' she said softly, 'before Sister Stewart sends out a search party.'

CHAPTER TWELVE

THE verdict turned out to be a flat refusal by an unrelenting consultant and an equally immovable Sister Stewart to discharge Eliot.

'There is nothing to stop me walking out,' he grumbled as he moved awkwardly from the bed where he had been examined to the chair.

Sister Stewart, overhearing him, glared back. 'Oh, yes, there is, Dr Powers. It's called common sense and if you have any left after that bang on the head, then I suggest you conserve it for your patients, who will doubtless see you soon enough.' She walked away, bristling, to follow the white-coated consultant who had refused to be intimidated by a colleague's bad-tempered protests.

'Damn cheek.' Eliot sat with his mouth open. 'Did you hear that?' Lauren was unsuccessfully trying to hide her laughter. 'What's so funny?' he demanded.

'You are—and your indignation at not having your own way. . .for once.'

'What do you mean, for once? I never have it at all with you.'

'I've not uttered a word.'

'But you want to. You want to say, I told you so.'

She sighed and sank to perch on the edge of his bed. 'Look, there would be absolutely no point in us driving back now, even if you were discharged. Mr Stone said he would see you in the morning. That means he's considering letting you go tomorrow. Just be patient.'

He shot her a frown. 'And what are you going to do for a bed tonight?'

'Sister Stewart has found me one in the nurses' quarters. But first I'm going to phone the practice and let them know the situation.' She left him to his brooding and phoned Hugo who, after he had heard her story, agreed to ring Shirley Viner.

When she returned to say goodnight to Eliot, he was so disgruntled that she stayed less than half an hour. Then she virtually dropped into her narrow borrowed bed and slept, surprisingly, very soundly until morning.

Washing, cleaning her teeth with a brush she had purchased from the shop and brushing her long dark hair until it shone and hung about her shoulders, she was daring to think that she might have escaped the usual sickness when her tummy heaved and the first wave of nausea hit her.

'You look shattered,' Eliot said as she arrived. 'And I don't doubt it if your night was anything like mine.'

'Stop complaining,' she told him unsympathetically. He was dressed, but crookedly, and must have had trouble with his sling, because it was sticking out from under his shirt, one loose sleeve swinging wildly, and his trousers were crumpled, with an oil mark spattered over them, obviously from the accident.

'Let's get out of here,' he said, dragging himself up.

'You've permission, I take it?'

'Damn it, of course I have.' He twisted his head towards the office. 'The old dragon has just gone off duty, but you'll find Staff there if you want to check.'

A lecture from Staff was the last thing Lauren felt like. And when she suggested a wheelchair he nearly had a fit and she watched him stubbornly stagger his way to the hospital foyer.

Once in the car he glared at the road, which was mushy with black snow. 'Watch out for the ice,' he commanded.

'There isn't any. There's been a thaw.'

'Do you know where you're going?' he barked as she peered at the signs.

'I do,' she retorted, losing her patience, and after a while she wound down the window to let in the air.

'What's the matter?' he asked, noticing. 'You've gone as white as a sheet.'

She pulled over to a lay-by and got out without answering and took herself off to recover. Five minutes later she reappeared and he was sitting there with a puzzled expression on his battered face. 'You haven't picked up a bug?' he said, and she started the car, shaking her head.

'Car sickness, I think.'

'First time I've ever known you to have that. Blessed nuisance not being able to drive,' he muttered, frowning at her. 'Lord knows where my car is. Police towed it away. Probably in a scrapyard by now.'

Lauren turned on the radio. It was playing jazz and she left it on, quite loudly, hoping it would shut up the miserable man.

An hour and fifteen minutes later they arrived in the dripping dampness of the Forest. This was the part she had been dreading. She pulled over at the roundabout and yanked on the handbrake.

'Why have we stopped? Are you sick again?' he asked.

'No. Where do you want me to take you?' She nodded to the choice of three roads.

'Might as well be the cottage,' he told her. 'I have to sort out some paperwork from my desk in the study. Insurance details, et cetera.'

She gritted her teeth, thrusting the gear into first, and headed the Saab off towards Gorsehall. Then the rain started in earnest and the heavens opened up and by the time they'd reached the cottage it was almost a torrent. They both sat in the car for a moment, staring at the rivers of rain cascading down the windscreen.

'Are you feeling any better?' he asked.

She nodded. The sickness had worn off, just.

'Let's get this over, then.'

She fiddled in her bag for the keys, hurried around to open the front door and was on her way back to help him out of the car when she almost collided with him.

'Come on,' he shouted through the rain, 'or you'll be soaked.'

Too late. She was soaked. They were both soaked. 'Hold still,' she said, and went up on tiptoe in the hall to peel off the drooping gauze on his forehead. She leant against him and felt his good arm slip around her and for a moment they rocked, until he steadied them both and asked roughly, 'Hadn't you better get rid of it?'

She nodded, looking down at the soaked pad in her fingers. 'I'll be in the kitchen if you need help.' And she moved clumsily out of his arms and found herself in the kitchen, staring blindly at the bin as she threw the pad away, and tore her eyes to the sink where she washed her hands.

The sensation of his body against her had upset her and she still felt weak from having to pretend that her breath hadn't caught in her throat and she hadn't ached violently for him.

The water became hot and she snatched back her hands and dried them, the sting making her realise she had better fill the moments with something useful to do until he found what he was looking for and walked out of her life for the last time.

The nausea, she realised thankfully, had turned into a niggling craving for odd foods. 'Strawberries,' she sighed, giving into the unreasonable fancy as she remembered a tin from the delicatessen hidden in the cupboard. Minutes later, she was standing at the sink, hunched over a treacly bowl of ruby-red strawberries, when Eliot walked in.

Guiltily she tried to hide the bowl amongst the washing-up debris, but he was too quick for her and made a face. 'Not strawberries?'

She looked up at him, her green eyes glinting like those of a cat who had just brought a frog into the house, unsure as to what to do with it. 'I was hungry,' she mumbled lamely.

'For those things? Five minutes ago you were complaining of nausea.' He pulled the bowl towards him, picked one out and munched it.

She licked her lips, watching the slow passage of it down his strong brown throat.

'Revolting,' he complained, but took another one all the same. Then very slowly he stopped munching and stared at her pink cheeks, which were gradually deepening into a blush. 'Strawberries for breakfast,' he muttered, as though he was talking to himself, 'and car sickness.'

Suddenly he stood motionless, one dripping fruit pinned between fingers halfway between bowl and mouth. His eyes seemed to flick downwards, then came back to land on her face, and she determinedly studied the dishes, turning over the washed cups that lay on the worktop.

'If I didn't know better. . .' he murmured, and drew a breath as she picked up a bone-dry cup and began drying it. 'If I didn't know better. . .'

'Tea?' she asked with shaky lips. 'Or have you finished in the other room?'

'If I didn't know better,' he pondered out loud for the third and final time, letting the strawberry plop back in the dish, 'I would say you are exhibiting some very extraordinary symptoms. . .'

'Tea it is, then.' She took two cups and saucers to the table as he followed her, watching her set them down as the cups jingled in their saucers, his tall body blocking her way as she turned.

'Eliot—'

He caught hold of her, sliding his arm around her waist and trapping her firmly against the sling. 'I'm not a complete idiot, you know, even with the bang on the head,' he said on a husky breath.

'I know you're not.' Suddenly she found she was locked into his dark gaze and her eyes were misting dangerously. 'It's not you who's the idiot. . .'

'Tell me,' he said, and her breath caught in her throat as a glistening wall of tears threatened to cascade over her lids.

'I can't,' she blubbered, and tried to push him away.

'You're pregnant, aren't you?'

She let out a funny little noise which sounded more like a distressed mouse and the tears plopped over as he groaned her name and shook her gently, his own breath held for a second as he took her head with his hand and kissed her tears away.

'Why didn't you tell me?'

'I didn't. . .I couldn't. . .'

'Why, Lauren? I am the father, aren't I?'

She burst into a fresh flood of tears and he pulled her head down on his chest, where she began to feel her weeping soak through his sling and onto his shirt. 'Of course you are,' she sobbed, 'but I didn't w-want you to feel trapped. To have to do the right th-thing. . .because I know you're involved with someone and I know you're moving to Oxford with her and with the way we've been—'

'You seem,' he cut in softly above her with a wonder-fully sexy hitch in his voice which rumbled through his chest and vibrated against her cheek, 'to know a lot about me that I don't know myself.'

He pressed a large white handkerchief into her hands
and she blew her nose and looked up at him. 'Do I?'
she mumbled, shuddering.

He bent down to lift her chin and tilted her mouth
gently to his as he murmured, 'You'd better come to
bed and tell me what else you know.'

His eyes were soft and seductive as he bent his head to
her height and took her in his good arm and pulled her
towards him and kissed her until she had to come up for
air, which was quite a feat for a man with a battered lip
and a redundant arm. She found the kiss so scrump-
tiously wonderful, tinged with rainwater and the earthy
fragrance of his scent, that she entwined her arms about
his neck and forgot all about Caroline and Oxford—and
the rest of the planet, come to that.

'Let's get out of these wet things,' he soothed her,
and she dragged herself away, vaguely aware that they
were in his room and he was staring at her strangely as
she slipped off her coat.

He sank onto the bed and she stopped undressing, her
fingers fumbling to a halt over her dress.

'Come here,' he said. 'I want to do that.'

'But you can't even undress yourself properly.'

'Can't I?' he chuckled. And, reaching over to pull her
down beside him, he growled, 'You seem to think you
know an awful lot about me.'

'Well, I should do. . .'

'Because we went to bed—once?' he taunted her, and
began to undo her buttons with five good, swift fingers.

'And look what happened on just that once.'

'It never occurred to me,' he murmured huskily, 'that
we would make babies. And I'm a doctor.'

'And so am I.' She giggled, slithering out of her dress,
and she began to help him with the sling first, careful

of the cast, and, peeling his shirt away, she let her eyes glide over the silky conker-brown skin beneath and its adornment of delicious dark hair.

'The one time,' he repeated, and pulled her back down as she stared at him, shivering slightly as he kicked off his shoes, slid out of the trousers and rolled cleverly beside her under the quilt.

She hugged him gingerly and he laughed and pulled her to him. 'I don't want to hurt you,' she sighed, and cupped his face in her hands. 'Be careful, you have so many wounds.' She shuddered as, as though to defy her, he released her bra and his mouth closed over one rosy bud and began to suck and tease, and she cradled him against her. 'Oh, Eliot. . .'

'I've wanted to make love to you for so long,' he breathed, fingering the soft, silky panties around her waist. 'Oh, God, how I do. It's been torture starting up at that blank ceiling in that dreadful bed.'

'But you weren't in hospital for more than a couple of nights,' she laughed softly.

'Not the hospital, clever clogs, the practice bed. Upstairs in that pitiful little cubby-hole we call the emergency room. Lord, it deserves its name.'

She stared at him, trying to make sense of the picture he had just drawn. 'You've been sleeping at the practice?'

'Where else? Where could I go in the village which wouldn't immediately reveal we'd had a darn great tiff and I'd walked out of my own house? Didn't you ever wonder why I arrived so early at work? I had to get up at the crack of dawn to avoid greeting our practice manager in my pyjamas.'

'But you don't wear pyjamas—'

'Precisely.'

She looked into his eyes and wondered how ever she could have not thought it out for herself, and suddenly she remembered the day when she had been feeling so ill just before she had helped him with Brian Searle and the removal of the mole.

'I saw your bag,' she murmured wonderingly. 'It was pushed into the corner and I thought you'd just put it there for the time being.'

'No such luck,' he chuckled, kissing the smooth skin behind her ear. 'Do you know, I got shaving and dressing down to such a fine art? I knew the exact moment the door would open downstairs and I'd fly down to wish the cleaners good morning, then disappear into my room looking as though it was the most natural thing in the world to have arrived there at seven every morning. That takes careful planning, you know.'

'But I thought you'd gone to Caroline's. I thought she had given up her job to move with you. . .'

He rolled her onto her back, growling under his breath as he shook his head. 'Can you honestly imagine me doing that? The girl's a perfect nuisance and you didn't help me any by making her so welcome. She actually thought you were playing Cupid, you miserable woman! And then when she delivered her little bombshell about finding a job in Oxford. . .'

'Oh, Eliot,' she breathed, and closed her eyes in aching relief. 'Oh, I'm sorry.'

'Too late now,' he told her, prising open her lips with his tongue and kissing her. 'Poor girl's packed her bags and gone.'

Lauren laughed sadly as she drew him down on her. She was sorry for Caroline, but she was so utterly relieved for herself. He lifted his head and stared at her, his dark eyes hungrily moving over her face and lingering on her open mouth. 'Tell me about our baby,' he whispered.

Lauren sighed, happiness beginning to seep into every part of her body, even her toes. 'I'm about nine weeks;

she's very small yet. I can't feel anything and I haven't put on any weight; that will come in the next few weeks, I expect.'

'A girl,' he said, and moved to lay his hand on her stomach and draw it gently over the valley between her hips. 'A girl, with her mother's beauty and her mother's eyes. Or a boy—'

'No,' Lauren whispered firmly, 'not a boy. I don't know how I know, but I do.'

'Well, this one's a girl. . .'

She slid her hands around his neck. 'Are you truly happy about her?'

He pulled her gently to him, locking their mouths together in a deep and longing embrace; her breath caught in her throat as he touched her and set her alight. 'How can I convince you?'

'More,' she told him. 'More of this.'

He slid between her thighs, and with a shuddering sigh began to move over her. The last thing she remembered before she fell headlong into paradise was that she should be careful of his arm, but even this thought diminished as he sighed her name and began to show her how much he loved her.

'Ready?'

'Ready.'

'You first.'

'No, you.'

'It's freezing out there. We forgot to put the heating on.'

Lauren dipped one toe into the ice-cold air and snatched it back under the quilt, wrapping herself around the warm body next to her.

He kissed the top of her head and nuzzled his mouth down to her throat. 'I'll go. In your condition—'

'My condition?' She giggled. 'Look at you. The walking wounded.' She closed her eyes, not wanting his lips to stop their downward journey. She hadn't thought of food since their return from hospital and now she was reluctant, in the middle of the night, to move.

'What have you got in the fridge?' he asked as he struggled from the sheets, curling one around him like a toga.

'Cheese if we're lucky. Biscuits if they aren't too soggy.'

'Stay where you are and keep warm.'

She snuggled back down into the warm nest and listened to him paddling downstairs, cursing as he bumped his arm on the dresser then whistling as he clattered happily in the kitchen. In ten minutes, he reappeared with a tray balanced against his chest and crept back in beside her.

They ate cheese and apple and two mountainous bowls of cornflakes and the saucer of strawberries, which Lauren refused to share.

When the tray was heaped with empty dishes and lowered to the floor, he turned to wrap her into him. She was silent for a moment, tracing the dark stubble of his jawline and letting her fingers linger on the small, healing cuts made by the glass in the accident. 'I could have lost you,' she murmured.

'I'm not that easy to get rid of.' He kissed her and she shuddered slightly at the thought.

'Eliot, what did Tom Clancey mean when he told me to ask you for the full story?'

'He said that?'

'He told me I should talk to you—he made me promise.'

'A promise you're only just keeping?'

She felt ashamed as she nodded, and he lay back, pressing her head into his shoulder. 'Before your finals, your mother came up to see me.'

'Mother? But she never said. . .' And Lauren realised suddenly why.

'She rang me first and we made a date for lunch. I think I had a suspicion of what was coming. Perhaps I was already feeling guilty.'

'For what, for heaven's sake?' She tried to lift her head, but he soothed her down again. 'We were in love. It wasn't a crime.'

'Let me finish. Your mother knew you were struggling with your studies—that much was evident from the number of times we kept turning up on her doorstep when you should have had your head down.'

'But, Eliot—'

'Listen.' He breathed deeply under her ear as though he was trying hard to say the right words and not hurt her. 'When we met, your mother was, as always, politeness itself. But her message was clear. You were young and on the very brink of the career you had always wanted. To expect you to make a commitment to me when you hadn't even begun to achieve what you had so long wanted in medicine was impossibly selfish. Even I could see that.'

'Did you want a commitment from me?'

'I told your mother I was going to ask you to marry me.'

Lauren closed her eyes and listened to his heartbeat. Her own heart seemed to throb in joy and sadness. After all this time, the words she had so longed to hear.

He kissed her hair, laying his cheek on her head. 'She asked me to think, very carefully, about what I was going to do. She said you would, she was sure, say yes. And she was also sure, if you didn't pass your finals, you would give up medicine and marry me, my darling, for all the wrong reasons. God help me, I didn't want to acknowledge the sense of what she said, but it was so absolutely true. In the end I agreed.'

'Oh, Eliot.'

'It was the hardest thing I ever had to do in my life.'

'But she didn't tell me!'

'If she had done, you would have thrown it all up, wouldn't you? We both knew that. In the end, all I could do was step out of your life.'

'And you think,' she mumbled miserably, 'I would have flunked my exams—if we had still kept seeing one another?'

He sighed above her. 'I couldn't take the chance. As your mother told me, if I loved you enough, I would set you free.'

'But I was so hurt, so abandoned. . .' she protested throatily.

'We thought we were doing what was best for you— for your future. And I, as your trainer, should have known better from the start. Rules are there for good reason.'

She knew it was true, but she still felt cheated. She had loved him so much. It wouldn't have been the end of the world if. . . Then she swallowed, trying to imagine just how she would have felt if she'd failed her finals. All the hard work. The years of dreaming. The desperation to succeed. . .

'Lauren, if it helps, your mother realised how unhappy we both were without one another. At least, when you'd gone to Africa, she realised. She suggested the idea for the partnership and I knew why. Before it was too late, she wanted to try to put things right in her own way.'

Lauren eased herself up in his arm and stared into the deep, deep blue eyes. 'Yes, I know. I received a letter from her, trying to explain. But she said nothing about selling you the cottage.'

He smiled gently, threading his fingers through her dark hair. 'Try to see it from her point of view. She thought the last thing you wanted was general practice, that Gorsehall might be a burden you didn't want. She was more aware of your need for independence, Lauren, than you ever gave her credit for. At the same time, she loved this house. I suppose she hoped this way. . .it might be kept in association with the practice. Who was to know what you would do—or want? She must have been torn.'

'Oh, Eliot,' she breathed, feeling the tears bubble over, and he pulled her into him, kissing her wet cheeks, his face hot on hers as she clung to him. 'I just wish I had come home. . .so we could have straightened things out. . .so she knew I would love this place as much as she did. . .I wish—'

'Shh,' he whispered, soothing her.

She was too full of emotion to reply. Instead she brought his face to hers and kissed him, running her tongue over the little puff of bruised lip which she had not helped by her lovemaking. His beard was rough and dark and the hollows of his eyes were still a faint purple, making the blue of the centres the kind of blue she always associated with stormy skies. She wanted to kiss all the storminess away, and as they slipped down together in the warmth of the bed she knew exactly how she would do it.

'September,' she whispered as she coiled herself around him carefully. She held his hand and drew it down over her tummy. Then she held it there for a few seconds as they waited breathlessly.

EPILOGUE

'I BAPTISE thee, Susan Lauren Kent. . .in the name of the Father and of the Son and of the Holy Spirit—'

Five-month-old Susan let out a healthy protest as a sparkling droplet of cold water ran into the dark cap of hair and trickled over her tiny ear. The vicar smiled and returned her swiftly to her mother.

Lauren gazed down at her baby with adoring green eyes and wondered if Susan's blue ones would change. She hoped not. She was so like Eliot as to make everyone quite unable to find a single feature that was her mother's. But of her paternity she was absolutely sure. Caesaren's were no mean feat—especially when your husband could tell you every stitch of it afterwards!

She gazed up at Eliot and read his eyes. 'Congratulations, Mrs Powers,' he bent to whisper, 'I love the both of you.'

Lauren flushed, so happy that she felt she must be glowing. How many women were fortunate enough to have the best of both worlds—Dr Lauren Kent still to her patients, Mrs Powers to the man who had slipped the slim band of gold on her finger a little over eleven months ago in this very church? Even now, she couldn't believe the dream! Still, look at the proof, she told herself incredulously, unable to think of anything more wonderful than having presented Eliot with a daughter.

After the service, outside St James's Parish Church, on the fine, crisp, sunny February morning a year after she had told Eliot he was going to be a father, she gazed

185

around the sea of familiar faces. There were, the Viners, George included, who had continued to recover, thanks to the kindness of Tom Clancey. And Tom himself, dressed today in a spanking new grey suit. The Freens and toddler Angela. Polly Sharp—a success story if there was ever one—was looking her old glamorous self once again. Then there were the Smiths, alias the Darbys—David, Chrissie and little Jasmine, three months older than Susan. And, holding her, Brian, her uncle who had been so worried about his benign mole and who was now accompanied by his young wife, Dawn, six months pregnant and under Lauren's care.

Ken Howard and his wife congratulated her then, followed by a disgracefully happy Hugo and his entire fleet of grandchildren. The girls from work gathered round, shamelessly adoring Susan, and Charles, over their heads, flashed a cheeky smile at her.

'No flirting,' Eliot said, bending over her shoulder when they were alone, 'with members of staff—or anyone else, come to that. You are a respectable married lady now.'

Lauren arched small, indignant dark brows. 'Indeed! Get thee to the kitchen, wench, is it?'

'No,' he whispered with an amused quirk of lips, 'to the marriage bed, my love, between thy fine satin sheets—'

Susan giggled and wrinkled her nose at them.

Lauren gazed up at him ruefully. 'She thinks you're funny.'

Eliot smirked as he gave her his finger. 'That's OK, just as long as her mother takes me seriously.'

Lauren refrained from answering, thinking how very much she would like to tell him at this very moment how desperately, mindlessly serious she was about him and always would be. But the man had an ego already— having just created this treasure in her arm, sometimes convincing himself, because Susan looked so much like him, that he was solely responsible for the miracle!

Susan raised her little white-mittened hands and giggled at her father again. They laughed with her and Eliot slid his hands around the beautiful white lace shawl and drew his daughter to his chest. Lauren's heart squeezed again at the sight.

'I hope we've more than a few tins of tuna and a few loaves to feed this little gathering,' Eliot muttered drily as the vicar came hurrying down the path.

Lauren giggled. 'What do you think I've been doing all morning whilst you've been swanning around Gorsehall, drinking tea in people's houses?'

'I've been on call!'

'A doctor's lot, I'm afraid.'

'Didn't think I'd get much sympathy. Besides, it's Sunday. . .why shouldn't I be offered a cup of tea?'

She linked her hand through the crook of his arm and wiggled Susan's toes. 'If you were to call on me, Dr Powers, say about half past eleven this evening, I might offer you many more interesting things than tea,' she whispered seductively, hoping the vicar couldn't lip-read as he flew towards them.

'Would you? What, for instance? Assuming I'm in the vicinity?'

'You'll have to wait until—'

'Mr and Mrs Powers! Now, I understand you've a little get-together planned at the cottage?'

Lauren and Eliot nodded in unison and Lauren squeezed her husband's arm tightly, to be rewarded with a flex of muscle. The vicar was referring to the christen-ing buffet but the get-together she was most looking forward to would be later, much later in the evening. When Susan was safely and contentedly asleep in the nursery after her last feed and, hopefully, there would be six or maybe even seven hours of undiluted peace, then she could snuggle up to the warm, strong body beside her and demonstrate exactly what she had in mind.

MILLS & BOON®

Medical Romance™

COMING NEXT MONTH

IF YOU NEED ME... by Caroline Anderson

Audley Memorial Hospital

Joe, now an Obs & Gynae consultant, had been fostered by Thea's parents so when, years later, she turned up on his doorstep, homeless and eight months pregnant, naturally he took her in. But behaving like a brother was difficult....

A SURGEON TO TRUST by Janet Ferguson

Anna's ex-husband had been a womaniser, and much as she liked working with surgeon Simon, she found it very hard to trust him, particularly when appearances suggested he might be just the same kind of man.

VALENTINE'S HUSBAND by Josie Metcalfe

Valentine dreaded her birthday, for it was her wedding anniversary too, a stark reminder of her husband and child, lost in a car accident. Escorting an old lady to France was the perfect escape, until she met Guy, a Casualty doctor, *and* Madame's grandson!

WINGS OF PASSION by Meredith Webber

Flying Doctors

After losing Nick, socialite Allysha had turned her life around and become a pilot for the RFDS, confident of her skills, but with no social life—until, quite unexpectedly, Nick arrived to replace Matt. How was she to convince him the change was real and lasting?

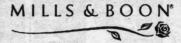

FREE!

FOUR FREE
specially selected
Medical Romance™ novels
PLUS a Mystery Gift
when you return this card...

Return this coupon and we'll send you 4 Medical Romance novels and a mystery gift absolutely FREE! We'll even pay the postage and packing for you.

We're making you this offer to introduce you to the benefits of the Reader Service™– FREE home delivery of brand-new Medical Romance novels, at least a month before they are available in the shops, FREE gifts and a monthly Newsletter packed with information.

Accepting these FREE books and gift places you under no obligation to buy, you may cancel at any time, even after receiving just your free shipment. Simply complete the coupon below and send it to:

MILLS & BOON READER SERVICE, FREEPOST, CROYDON, SURREY, CR9 3WZ.

No stamp needed

Yes, please send me 4 free Medical Romance novels and a mystery gift. I understand that unless you hear from me, I will receive 4 superb new titles every month for just £2.10* each, postage and packing free. I am under no obligation to purchase any books and I may cancel or suspend my subscription at any time, but the free books and gift will be mine to keep in any case. (I am over 18 years of age)

M7XE

Ms/Mrs/Miss/Mr _____

Address _____

_____

_____ Postcode _____